THREE STEPS CLOSER TO DEATH

Bill Gary strolled up closer and closer to the spot where the wolf lay with the wind ruffling his fur. He came within three steps, within two, within one.

And then the heap of fur twitched into life. Bill Gary had a chance to heave up the ax, but he was far too late to spring back. The slash of the knife-sharp fangs caught him across the inside of his right thigh and cut through the tough cloth of his trousers, and into the deep, soft flesh — cutting and tearing . . .

*Books by Max Brand
from The Berkley Publishing Group*

THE BIG TRAIL
BORDER GUNS
CHEYENNE GOLD
DAN BARRY'S DAUGHTER
DEVIL HORSE
DRIFTER'S VENGEANCE
THE FASTEST DRAW
FLAMING IRONS
FRONTIER FEUD
THE GAMBLER
GOLDEN LIGHTNING
GUNMAN'S GOLD
THE GUNS OF DORKING HOLLOW
THE LONG CHASE
LOST WOLF
MIGHTY LOBO
MONTANA RIDES
MYSTERY RANCH
THE NIGHTHAWK TRAIL
ONE MAN POSSE
OUTLAW BREED
OUTLAW'S CODE
THE REVENGE OF BROKEN ARROW
RIDERS OF THE SILENCES
RUSTLERS OF BEACON CREEK
SILVERTIP
SILVERTIP'S CHASE
THE STRANGER
TAMER OF THE WILD
TENDERFOOT
TORTURE TRAIL
TRAILIN'
TRAIL PARTNERS
WAR PARTY

SILVERTIP'S CHASE

B

BERKLEY BOOKS, NEW YORK

This Berkley book contains the complete text
of the original edition.

SILVERTIP'S CHASE

A Berkley Book / published by arrangement with
G. P. Putnam's Sons

PRINTING HISTORY
Warner edition / November 1973
Berkley edition / January 1990

ISBN: 0-425-11973-4

A BERKLEY BOOK ® TM 757,375
Berkley Books are published by The Berkley Publishing Group,
200 Madison Avenue, New York, New York 10016.
The name "BERKLEY" and the "B" logo
are trademarks belonging to Berkley Publishing Corporation.

PRINTED IN THE UNITED STATES OF AMERICA

10 9 8 7 6 5 4 3 2

CHAPTER I

Frosty

FROSTY was perfect. He had the hazel eyes of a fighter, eyes that became whirling pools of fire when a kill was at hand. He was heavily muscled where strength was needed, and yet there was not an extra ounce for him to carry when it meant traveling fast and far. One looked at him as one always looks at a fighter, seeing first shoulders, jaw, and eyes. And there was nothing that should be changed.

Frosty was perfect, because he could kill anything that was able to catch him. He was perfect because he could keep himself warm in winter and cool in summer by natural alterations. He was perfect because he knew how to feed himself. He was perfect because he was in the first young prime of his life, and the world had not yet scarred and hurt him; neither had this universe ceased being a great mystery to him.

Frosty was a timber wolf, or buffalo wolf, or lobo, or any one of a dozen other terms. But he was dignified with a name that had appeared in the public print more than once. That was because he had discovered, when he was still a gaunt, leggy yearling, that veal is easy to kill and delicious to the taste. He began killing young cattle when he was scarcely a year old, and then he kept on killing them.

Frosty was not confined to one diet, as a matter of fact. He knew only one thing—that the majority of meats produced by man's care are tenderer than the meats produced by a wild life. Therefore Frosty spent a great deal of his time within sight and sound and scent of man.

If it happened that the tender-throat calves were too well protected inside the herd, Frosty knew all about the ways of approaching chicken houses. He could rear from the floor and take a rooster off its perch without giving the poor fowl a chance to flap its wings once before it was dead. He knew how to get into a barn and hunt out the chickens there. Once he had actually got up on the hay-mow and picked off some pigeons on their nests among the upper rafters.

But there were other things to be found within sight and sound of man. There were rabbits—not the long, stringy jacks such as he was accustomed to snap up on the desert or in the mountains by dint of work of the brain, never by speed of foot—but fat, thick-fleshed rabbits even one of which made quite a meal! There were tiny little items such as caged squirrels, whose wire cages could be bashed open by the stroke of a heavy forepaw. And near the house of man one could find goats staked out on a convenient rope—if it were in a town—and stupid yearling calves standing in corrals.

He knew where at least half a dozen farmers' wives had their creameries in which broad pans of milk were standing, and where eggs accumulated in deep dishes. He knew how to clip the end off an egg and swallow the contents without the shell as expertly as any fox with delicate muzzle. He knew how to nose or paw open a door and lap up the milk in the pans. He knew how to visit coolers of a summer night, coolers of burlap with water dripping over them from pans at the top. Cold meats, butter, and various delicacies were contained in those coolers—and sometimes summer may be a hungry season.

Frosty knew the taste of fresh pork, and he loved it. Pigs were easy to kill. It was a question of running very low and catching the porker with the shoulder so that the fat beast fell on its back. Then one knife slash of the long fangs and the throat was open and the life was streaming out.

It was just a neat little trick, because pigs were not easy to kill for some predatory animals. Their weight was too close to the ground, and their teeth were too sharp, their jaws too powerful. But it was true that most affairs in this life could be made smooth by the use of tricks.

There was plenty of sheer brawn in Frosty. He was the biggest timber wolf that had ever terrorized the cattlemen of the Blue Water Mountains. He had, in fact, a spread of foot that was so huge that those who were not initiated could hardly believe that it was the tread of a wolf at all. A hundred-and-ten-pound wolf is a big fellow; but Frosty weighed a hundred and fifty—not hog-fat, but in the height of good running condition. But for all of his bulk, he knew that brains are better than toothwork.

He had had a wise mother to teach him things in the beginning. And he had a mind that was able to improve on what he learned from others. He knew that squirrels bury nuts, because he had seen them dig up part of the treasure. And a wolf may enjoy nuts in a hungry hour. He knew most expertly that rabbits may be worn out to a frazzle without much effort on the part of the hunter, because a startled rabbit will run a mile like a winging arrow, gradually turning as it runs, unless pressed too hard. A wise wolf stays in the center of the circle and keeps starting the jack until it is exhausted.

Once from a distance he had watched an old Southern hound kill a wild cat after walking around and around it until the nervous cat was brain tired and nervously limp. He had tried the same method with perfect success.

He had seen a pack of four wolves pull down a bull after hamstringing it. Well, what the pack could do, one wolf might manage. No bull on the range can turn fast enough to keep away an active wolf, and, once behind the big fellow, it is not hard to cut the huge tendon that runs down the back of the leg. One hamstring gone and the other will soon follow. Then the bull must fall, and the wolf may dine.

He knew a great many other things.

There was man, for instance.

Man is the great enemy that must not be faced. One may treat a mountain lion, or even the terrible, sage grizzly bear, almost with contempt—if one has four fast feet and good terrain to use them over. But man is different. He is accompanied by the scent of iron and powder, always. He makes a noise from a distance and hurls through the air an invisible tooth that Frosty had seen bite a huge elk to death at a single stroke. Frosty had seen a monstrous grizzly bear smitten to the ground, not by a single noise, but by several. He had seen the hair of the bear fly where one of the invisible teeth grazed its back.

Moreover, Frosty had had those same teeth go by him in the air. Once he had heard the hum of one in the air and heard the sound of the tooth going through a sapling close to him. Afterward he came back and sniffed the hole through the tree. It was clean cut. It bored straight through. Not the greatest bear that ever lived could bite like that; not the great god of bears could do such damage!

Man, also has many devices. He puts on the ground raw meat, fresh and delicious, but with a peculiar scent adhering. Wolves that eat this meat die. Frosty's own mother had died in this manner. Man also puts, here and there through the brush, entrancing scents, and if a wolf comes close to them, a steel mouth bites upward from the ground and then closes on the wolf's leg.

Frosty had been fighting with a big, mature he-wolf one day, and the steel teeth had struck upward from the ground and caught his enemy.

Afterward Frosty learned never to trust strange scents.

The very truth is that Frosty loved to learn almost as much as he loved to eat.

But his appetite was also very good, and he liked frequent meals. Your average wolf will gorge at a kill. But Frosty learned better after he had been twice hunted by Major Tweedale's pack of wolfhounds. Major Herbert

Tweedale had the best pack of hounds in the Blue Water Mountains, and it was his boast that they never failed to get their prey.

He had made that boast before he encountered Frosty. The major learned something then; the hound pack—except for two which Frosty killed—learned something, also; and Frosty learned most of all. He learned that a filled belly may bring an early death.

Frosty dined temperately, but always on the choicest morsels. Or perhaps he learned to appreciate a lean figure, because he was never so starved that he was tempted to swell himself with food. Famine never came anywhere near Frosty. He liked warm food. He liked it fresh. He never returned to a dead carcass.

And that was why the ranchers had placed upon his famous head a bounty of no less than two thousand dollars!

Yes, more than the bounty on the head of many a murderer! But who can blame them when it is remembered that Frosty, day after day, all through the year, descended from the heights above timber line, killed fresh beef, ate sparingly thereof, and retired again?

Guns could not harm him now, because he had learned that guns do not bite at night any more than birds sing.

Poison could not harm him, because he would not eat cold meat.

Traps could not catch him, because the scent of steel seemed to rise before him out of the ground like a red danger signal.

For all of that, Frosty was to be caught in a trap on this winter day when the wind was blowing white streamers of snow powder off the tops of the Blue Waters. He was to be caught by the cleverest trapper that ever worked in that district. And yet, strangely enough, though Bill Gary was particularly hunting Frosty for the great bounty, it was only by accident and second chance that the famous wolf was snared.

Because of that accident, Bill Gary died without ever collecting the bounty he wanted, and Jim Silver rode into the strangest of all his adventures.

CHAPTER II

Bill Gary's Discovery

BILL GARY did nothing but trap wolves. He cared little about other pelts, even the precious fur bearers. What he knew about was wolves, and what he wanted was wolves and nothing else.

He looked as though he had been born to his work, because he greatly resembled a wolf in his own person. He had a great, shaggy head and heavy shoulders. He had a slouching gait, a bright and dangerous eye, and the manners of an eater of raw meat.

There was nothing good to be said about Bill Gary, except that he knew how to catch wolves. Otherwise he was a huge, snarling, sullen, dangerous boor. He never went down to a town except to collect his bounties, lay in a supply of bacon, flour, a few other necessaries, and perhaps a new trap or two. He never stayed in a town longer than one whisky drunk and a few fights.

After some of those fights the oher fellow was crippled for life. Bill Gary fought foul, because that was his nature. He never saw any point in giving the other fellow a chance, any more than Frosty would have dreamed of giving a tender young beef a chance for its life when he was hungry. Bill Gary fought because he loved to give pain, just as Frosty fought because he wanted fresh meat.

Bill Gary had traveled a thousand miles to come to the range of Frosty. The fame of the great wolf had traveled far and wide during the last year, but when it came to the ears of Bill Gary that such a small fortune could be collected for the scalp of a single wolf, when he heard moreover that this wolf could be known by the mere spread of its foot, and that it had its name from its pale-gray, misty color, he could hardly wait to pack his traps on a mule and start south. So he got to the Blue Waters, heard as much as he needed to know about the range of the monster, and went out to catch him.

Bill Gary arrived in October. This was March—a white, cold, windy March in the upper mountains—and still Gary had not so much as laid an eye on the great wolf. He had caught several others, but he had not so much as glimpsed the cattle eater.

Nearly any other man would have given up the task long before and attributed his lack of success to the work of the devil. But Bill Gary was as stubborn as steel, and therefore he remained at his work.

On this day, with a burden of No. 4½ Newhouse traps —the only traps ever specially designed for the catching of timber wolves—Bill Gary trudged through the Blue Waters above the timber line.

He bore with him, also, a strong ax, with a head wide and heavy enough to serve for the driving of stakes, and he had with him a big chunk of fresh venison to serve as bait.

So weighted down, it was a hard pull for Bill Gary up the snowy slopes, but he minded no labor when he was working at his favorite occupation. He came now to the crest of a ridge where the wind had scoured the snow away; there, on a rock ledge, he sat down to rest himself while his eye ran over the picture of the great, gaunt mountains, blue-white against the gray of the sky. Below extended the forest of pines, dark as night, and the plains and foothills beyond were lost in the winter mist. Out of a canyon near by he heard the calling voices of a torrent so strong that even the winter had been unable to silence it.

None of these things had an important meaning to Bill Gary. He simply wished that the spring would hurry along, because spring is the best season, as every one knows, for the trapping of wolves. Now, when the ache had disappeared from behind his knees, he stood up and stretched himself. He saw a knob of rock jutting from the ledge, and he struck it an idle blow with the back of his ax, breaking it off short. Then he strode on.

But after he had gone a step or two, he began to think of something that his eyes had seen, but which had had no meaning to his mind at the moment.

He turned, went back, and at this instant the cloud opened, and a flare of sunshine fell right on the ledge of rock.

There was little superstition in Bill Gary, but it seemed to him that a bright, glorious hand had reached down from the sky to point to and gild his good fortune.

For there was no doubt of the thing that glittered from the broken face of the ledge. It was a dark stone on the outside, but within the skin of weathering it was gray with a crystal glittering. There was another brightness that matched and overmatched the sun that fell on it—a veining of yellow, of shining yellow!

Bill Gary looked suddenly and wildly around him. If there had been another man in sight, it would have gone ill with the stranger. But there was no one near. Who *would* enter this white wilderness at this season of the year?

Suddenly it seemed to Gary that this was his reward from whatever mysterious powers may be. It was his repayment for the long years of service which he had spent in wiping from the face of the earth as many as possible of the four-footed meat eaters. Here was the exchange which fate gave him—gold!

Perhaps it was only a point, a spot?

He took ten steps down the ledge and struck with the back of the ax again. A weighty fragment broke away—and again the glorious yellow glittered up at him!

He suddenly saw himself in a great, roaring city, and the great city was his. The roar of it was as the voice of his power. He saw an army of faces, and they belonged to him. He would be rich. He would be as rich as Midas!

He began to laugh, for he was thinking of his nephew, that poor, hard-working cow-puncher, Alec Gary, who drudged from year to year trying to save enough money to marry the girl of his choice. Well, what would Alec think when his savage uncle descended from the mountains with both hands filled with gold?

After laughing at Alec, after taunting him, Bill Gary decided that he might even give a little charity to his nephew, because, after all, Alec was not a bad sort of a lad. He kept his mouth shut, he never criticized, and he knew how to work. And, after all, his name was Gary. Bill Gary, the black sheep, might now become the head of the family, the man to whom the whole tribe looked up for advice, and for help. Well, some of the advice that he had in mind to give them would work under the skin and sting them to the bone, if he knew his own mind!

He took out a pencil and a notebook. He was a methodical fellow, and he was old enough as a hunter to understand that one may forget one's place in the wilderness. So he wrote down a description in the notebook, after he had unwrapped it from the piece of oiled silk which protected it from moisture.

Thunder Mountain on the right; Chimney Peak on the left. I face Mount Wigwam. A ledge of black rock outcropping.

That was enough for him. He could always locate the place from that description.

But how deep did the vein run? Was it only a surface skimming, or did it go down deep?

Well, he had a double jack and a drill down in his cabin, and the shack was only a mile away. He would soon make out the truth—at least he would cut a little deeper into it.

So he put down the load of fresh meat and traps and the ax. It would be a joke on him, he thought, if a wolf happened by and ate that bait before a trap was set! Then he strode off down the slope toward the cabin.

13

"Cabin" was too much of a name for it. Some unknown man had built it, perhaps the year before. It was a crazy little shack that leaned against a rock, but it had the advantage of running water near by, and, of course, plenty of wood for fuel. It was good enough for Bill Gary, who used to be fond of saying that his own hide was tent enough to shelter him from winter.

As he came through the trees his two dogs jumped up. They had been lying on either side of the entrance to the shack, and now they sprang up and stared at him with their wistful, red-stained eyes. Neither of them made a sound. They had been trained to hunt silently, fight silently, die silently, if need be.

Perhaps they had no desire to give tongue when they saw their master, for they had no love for him. To him they were simply tools. To them he was simply a resistless and cruel force which must be obeyed. Of their own kind, they were magnificent. He had bred them for his own purposes in hunting wolves. He had bred them big, on a basis of greyhound and Scottish deerhound for speed and general conformation. He had dashed in some mastiff to give ferocity, and some St. Bernard and Great Dane for size. For fifteen years he had been creating these monsters, and now he had a pair, either one of which was capable of giving a wolf a hard tussle single-handed.

Shock weighed a hundred and eighty pounds. Tiger was a good deal bigger. When he stood up on his hind legs his head was almost a foot above that of his master. They were as ugly as nightmares, but they had the qualities for which the master had bred them—wind, speed, and a tenacious love of battle at all times.

They had Red Cross collars around their necks. Big Bill Gary grinned as he considered that name for them. He had bought them because they were made of rustless, hinged plates of steel, so broad that they would be useful—and had indeed proved useful—in parrying the slash of a wolf when it cuts for the throat. But originally they had been Red Cross collars for use on big trained dogs that could go among the wounded, perhaps, and carry first-aid kits. Each collar had, also, a little flat compartment under one

14

of the steel plates. It closed with a strong snap, and was almost air-tight. That was for messages that the injured could write when they used the dog to send out a call for help. That was why Bill Gary grinned—when he thought that those collars had been made for purposes of mercy, and he had put them on his killers.

He had a pair of pack harnesses for the dogs, too. He put one of them on Shock and loaded the heavy double jack onto it. He put a pair of drills and some fuse and blasting powder on Tiger. He decided that he ought to saddle the dogs more often and take them out to carry burdens. It hardened them. It made them a little slower, but it hardened them for the struggle of a fight.

Now he was prepared to go back to that ledge above him and tackle the problem of what it contained. So he strode away again, with the two great dogs following him. They went actively up the steepness of the slope, arching their backs high, sticking out their long tongues as they panted. One shifty red eye was always fixed upon him. He saw that and liked it. He always liked it. He would rather have either beast or man fear than love him.

When he got up to the ridge, he scowled back at the line of tracks which extended behind him. He was a fool to have come so straight. He should have wandered off to the side and buried his sign as he went. However, the sky was turning gray, and snowflakes were falling.

He forgot the trail and went to his work. In his powerful hand the heavy, twelve-pound double jack plied as easily as a single jack in the grasp of an ordinary man. It drove the bit chunking rapidly into the rock. He drilled a hole not too deep, slanting it up under a big and massive projection of the ledge. Then he put in a shot of powder, buried the fuse, and lighted it. From the near distance he waited, sitting down cross-legged, and heard the hollow boom of the report. He thought at first that the explosion had simply "bootlegged." Now he returned to find that it had in reality neatly cracked off the outthrust of the rock. A two-hundred-pound mass lay on the ground, and right across the heart of it lay the precious golden streakings.

He looked up sharply, savage as a beast from a meal

of raw meat. The wind, in a strong gust, blew a flurry of snow into his face. He was glad of the cold beat of the wind. He was glad to take the force of the blast, because it assured him that no other men were likely to be near.

He thought of covering up the ledge. But no, there was no use of that. A falling of trees to cover the places where he had broken the stone would simply call the attention of any traveler. And if he heaped snow over the exposure, the wind would scour it away.

Well, other men could thank their lucky stars that they did not come to bother him just now!

He licked his chapped lips as he stared at the veining of the gold. It was all his. He felt the running of the gold in the vein as he felt the running of the blood in his body. He felt able to chew the gold out of the rock.

Then, as he looked about him, he took note of the venison which still had not been used.

He had found a gold mine, to be sure, but that did not by any means eradicate his sense of the months which he had spent in the pursuit of the great Frosty. It merely freed his hands to devote his full artistry to the task of catching the famous wolf. He determined, before he started on the long trek to town to file on his claim, that he would first of all take a last chance to catch Frosty.

So he turned his back on the ledge and went on up the slope.

CHAPTER III

Tragedy Planned

No MAN'S common sense continues when he has to deal with the thing he loves. If Bill Gary had consulted his common sense, he would have gone straightway to file his claim, but instead of using his matter-of-fact brain, he remembered that he loved wolf trapping. That was what caused trouble for Frosty. That was why the great Barry Christian was hurled into danger, and why Jim Silver rode strange trails for a long time. Also, that was how Bill Gary came to die.

He left his dogs well behind him when he found what he wanted, which was an open place in the woods, higher up the slope. There was even a little knoll in the middle of the opening, which made the thing perfect, and the snow was not lying on the ground; there was only a sheathing of dead, brown pine needles.

The big, fresh, crimson chunk of venison he hung eight feet from the ground on the branch of a tree at the edge of the clearing.

He did not put the trap on the ground under the tree, because a careful timber wolf that knows anything about the arts of the trapper is fairly sure to suspect just such a device. And a wolf which will make a hundred-yard detour around a blaze on a tree has such hair-trigger sensitiveness of nose and eye that it is fairly sure to find the human hand wherever it has appeared, once it is roused to the search.

Gary cut three six-foot stakes, each with a strong crotch at one end. He took three Newhouse traps. Each had a long chain attached to it, and at the end of each chain there was a ring. He passed the rings over the ends of the stakes and drove them into the ground on or near the little knoll in the center of the clearing. In the end, each chain was securely anchored in this fashion, and the stake was driven down until the head of it as well as the crotch was out of sight.

The three traps were then placed on the knoll and covered over with fresh pine needles. Those needles were not taken from the spot. They were brought from a distance, and they were handled with pieces of bark, so that the scent which exudes from the hands of a man might taint the air as little as possible. All to the eye and to the scent must be as undisturbed as possible in appearance.

When he had finished setting the traps, Bill Gary moved off to a distance, called his dogs, and strode off up the mountainside to visit a similar set of traps which he had arranged two days before. He was well out of sight before the tragedy which he had planned actually began.

A big lop-eared wolf running across the mountain suddenly dropped to his haunches and pointed his nose into the wind. For down that wind came the eloquent tale of red meat. Lop-ear was a good hunter, an expert hunter. But he was not in a class with the great Frosty. Therefore his belly, at certain seasons, cleaved close to his backbone, and this was one of the seasons. Hunting had been bad. It had been terribly bad, and the call of the red meat was frightfully strong in him.

So he went up the wind to find the treasure. He did not run in a straight line, but shifting here and there, his nose high and then low. For there were some odd features about the scent of that meat. The odor was fresh as that of a yearling deer, and yet the odor was not hot. At any rate, the delicious scent was not retreating. He took his time about the stalking, therefore, and it was some minutes later before he ventured to thrust his nose out from the edge of the clearing.

He dropped to his belly at once, his hair bristling with fear. For man had been there. There was unmistakable evidence in the heavy air close to the ground, that man had been there not very long before. But, for that matter, man was everywhere in the woods, and in a great many portions of the white district above the timber line, even. Here, where he was close to the upper verge of the trees, the wolf was not so accustomed to meeting the dreadful scent. That was why he remained still for a long time before he ventured forward.

He could not only smell the prize, but he could see it, now. It hung red as a jewel in the branch of a tree.

Could he reach it? It seemed just on the verge of his jumping powers! He retreated, took a strong run, and then checked himself shortly on skidded legs that trembled with fear. For he had remembered that the ground he was to land on might not be secure. Therefore he checked himself and began to sniff carefully. His eyes became dim as the intensity of his search increased. What good are eyes for near hunting, compared to the powerful concentration of a wolf's power of smell?

He found the ground clear. It was not clean, to be sure, for the horrible smell of man was on it, but it was clear of all actual danger, as far as Lop-ear could make out.

So he ran back to the proper distance, ran forward, and hurled himself high into the air.

His teeth clicked only a few inches beneath the prize.

He went back again. His eyes were red-stained with passionate desire now, and his mouth was drooling. Again, again, he drove himself as high as he could into the air.

Then, standing back for another try, he measured the leap and told himself that he could never manage the thing. His brain was strong enough to give him that clear assurance; and therefore he retreated after the manner of his kind to the first high place in the clearing, and sat down and lifted his voice in mourning. If he had found a vast bull moose or an elk bogged in the snow and had been afraid of tackling the monster himself, he would have sat down in the same fashion and sent up the same wild, long-drawn, unearthly howl. Every wolf within miles, hearing it, would know that it meant just one thing: "Red meat to be had! Red meat to be had!" And they would come. They could hardly resist coming.

He sat down and howled, and his cry reached the ears of a far greater and wiser wolf in the distance—Frosty, that sleek and untroubled robber of farmyards on the one hand and the wilderness on the other.

In what a complicated way Fate was working against Frosty, using in part the skill of the trapper and in part the wiles of Frosty's own kind! Hardly had Frosty heard that first long wail when the voice of Lop-ear snapped off into silence; for as he shifted back in giving his yell a greater volume, he had done what Bill Gary expected, and put his foot into a trap that shut its strong teeth of steel into the flesh and tendons of the leg and bit down toward the bone.

But Frosty could not tell that. All he knew was that there had been one wolf cry of such a volume that it announced the presence of a he-wolf of almost, if not quite, his own proportions. If that were the case, the fellow had to be thrashed or killed.

Frosty turned with joy on the trail of a fight and ran with winged feet down the wind to get at the stranger. It was his duty, and it was his pride, to keep his own run as clear of other wolves as he could. If he had resided constantly among the mountains, he would have kept the marches of his domain as free from other wolves as the parlor table of a good housewife is free from dust. But Frosty made so many and such long excursions in the dangerous lowlands, where the habitations of man were thick, that he did not keep his kingdom properly policed. He was all the keener, therefore, to get at the stranger.

As for fighting, he knew all about it. There was hardly a night, during his travels from village to village and from ranch to ranch, when he did not run into whole packs of dogs. Some of them would run at the mere scent of a wolf. But others were his full equal in size and had been bred to the work. Therefore Frosty was kept efficient in the cunning fence of tooth and shoulder with which a wolf lays his peers low.

He knew how to shift his big weight like a shadow, feinting here and there. He knew how to strive for a hamstring as well as for the throat, which was the limit of fighting sense of many wolves. He knew, even—and dogs had taught him this—that a leg hold, maintained half a second with due wrenchings, would probably break the bone. He knew that when the other fellow has been overturned by a charge there is always the belly as a larger and easier target. A wound there may be as fatal, though not so quickly.

One might consider Frosty, in fact, not so much as a mere sneak thief, as he could be held a bold pirate that cruised through dangerous waters and constantly defied the attacks of whole fleets of armed ships of war. And this was certainly true: that more than almost any other of his kind, he had the sort of pride that makes a warrior stand and fight instead of running away, even from overwhelming odds.

There was one occasion when he had driven a whole pack of five wolves from the freshly killed carcass of an elk; not that he needed the meat, but because he wanted to see what a mixture of bluff, courage, and fighting skill could accomplish.

This was the Frosty that you must have in mind as he hurried down the wind to find the meaning of that voice which had dared to give tongue in the midst of his realm. Imagine him as a great form of misty gray, swiftly running, with his head high, since there was no scent for him to follow.

He was almost on top of the clearing before the scent of man struck him like the pealing sound of a rifle. The scent doubled him up and turned him around. He skirted rapidly, furtively, around the clearing, and on the farther side of it he found the trail of the big wolf which had come there before him. Moreover, the wind carried to him two smells of blood. One was venison; one was that of a wounded wolf.

It was very intriguing. It was just the sort of a scent that one might expect to come across where a wolf had succeeded in pulling down a deer and had been wounded in the struggle.

On his belly, Frosty pulled himself through the brush and came out on the verge of the open, and there he had sight of a figure which made him bristle the hair of his mane and rise slowly to his feet, with glaring eyes.

For there on the knoll in the middle of the clearing lay a huge wolf. Yes, a monster almost of his own proportions. The head of the stranger was turned toward him. His snarling lips unmasked fangs of terrible proportions.

What amazed Frosty was that the stranger did not deign to rise to meet him. It was as though the big fellow preferred to keep his gaze fixed on the bit of red meat that dangled in the branches of the pine tree to the right. Poor fool, could he not tell that that meat must have been placed there by the hand of man?

Observe the cruel workings of fate against Frosty! If the trapped wolf had risen an instant sooner, if there had been the slightest sight or jangling sound of the steel chain, if there had been the least suspicion of a trap, Frosty would have given that place a berth miles wide. But as it was, he was merely overwhelmed with rage at what he considered the contemptuous indifference of the stranger.

Left to his own cunning, Frosty would have detected every trap that even Bill Gary could have placed for him. Already for six months he had been avoiding them. But now, half blinded by rage, he hurled himself straight at the enemy. He reached the knoll. And as he reached it, as the stranger rose, too late Frosty saw the glitter of the deadly chain and the trap that was attached to a foreleg of Lop-ear. For in that very instant, as he tried to put on the brakes, Frosty jammed his left hind foot right into a Newhouse trap!

CHAPTER IV

Battle and Death

THE charge of Frosty had brought him well within the leaping distance of Lop-ear. That big fellow was a fighter on his own account, with plenty of wolf experience behind him. He went right in, low and hard, and got a tooth parry for his pains.

A tooth parry is executed by a wolf that knows its business and trusts the strength of its teeth. It is a slashing stroke, not at the body, but at the striking mouth of an enemy. Lop-ear, with slashed lips, shrank back from that strange shock, and as he shrank, Frosty jumped in and gave him the shoulder thrust. The full weight of his big body was behind that blow, and Lop-ear immediately dropped over on his back.

He never rose again. It was as though a sword had opened his throat with a slashing blow. The grip of Frosty finished the battle there and then.

But the instant Lop-ear was dead, the limp body became of no importance. Those other teeth of steel which were fastened in the hind leg of Frosty were what mattered. He sat down and studied what had happened.

The grip did not grow less. Once a bulldog had clamped down on his leg and kept working in its teeth to break the bone. That was the way this skeleton jaw of death, this grisly and cold monster, locked its grip on the leg of Frosty.

Suddenly he pointed his nose at the sky, and a howl worked up in his throat, a yell of despair. That sound was never uttered. He had learned during long process of time that noise makes no matter better in the wilderness. It can bring trouble, but never help.

Therefore Frosty swallowed the yell of pain, the appeal for sympathy. Instead, he turned his head once more and considered the only possible way of escape. He got up and tentatively pulled until the chain was tight. There was no give to it. He went over and studied the way the chain disappeared into a narrow hole in the ground. Buried in that hole was wood. That was as far as the intelligence of Frosty could solve the mystery. The iron came like a snake out of the ground, and the bodiless jaws were attached to the chain.

Yet there was another resource.

He could not free himself with a sound body, but he could escape by maiming himself. He could gnaw off the foot that was imprisoned in the grasp of the trap. Already the leg was numb below the point where the steel teeth were fastened upon him.

He was about to grind his powerful teeth through the bones of his own leg when there was another interruption.

Up the hillside, far away, Bill Gary had heard the mournful wail of Lop-ear some time ago. His dogs had heard it, also, and had been anxious to run toward the sound. But Gary, as he turned and countermarched, kept them at hand. It was only when he was comparatively close to the clearing that he allowed the big, savage brutes to cut loose and run ahead toward the silence of the traps.

And now Frosty saw them lurching through the brush and out into the open. He stood up. Pain from his wound hunched his back. Hatred and loathing of these enemies made his hair bristle. They were huge. Either of them might make a formidable antagonist, even if his feet were free for maneuvering in the battle. The two together would probably tear the life out of him, and he knew it.

Frosty despised his fate. There had been nobler ways of dying, as when the great grizzly almost cornered him one day, or as when the dog pack in the village had actually tumbled him off his feet. But now, against only two dogs, to be found pinned down to the ground, helpless.

He stood there rigid, glaring. The horrible scent of man blew to him from the reeking bodies of the dogs. They were man-made engines of battle, and he hated them with the religious hatred of the wilderness.

They knew their work, this pair. Tiger circled immediately around to the rear and charged. Shock came in from the front.

For that frontal attack Frosty apparently braced himself, acting as though he intended to abandon his hind quarters to the second enemy until he had disposed of the first attacker. But that was not at all what he had in his cunning mind.

Truly and strongly, Shock rushed in to carry his charge home as Tiger flashed in from the rear, but from the corner of his eye Frosty gauged the proper instant. Then he wheeled and struck.

Tiger tried to dodge. In trying to dodge, he naturally lifted his head a little. That was why Frosty found the most perfect target that a wolf could ask for, and flashed both his fangs in the soft under throat of Tiger.

Shock, overcharging his target that had shifted so suddenly, made a flying snap that laid open the haunch of Frosty. Then, as Shock turned, he saw his companion standing back, coughing blood, and standing on legs that were already beginning to tremble at the hocks and knees.

A wiser dog than Shock might have realized that, for all his size and strength, he was not capable of meeting this master of fight. But Shock was not wise, really. His eyes were red, and in his brain there was no knowledge except that of battle. He had been bred to fly at the enemy. He was hurled by the will of his absent master, like a javelin at the mark. So he plunged straight in at Frosty.

For Frosty it was child's play now. He stood erect and

huge till the instant of the contact. Then he dropped flat to the ground and slashed upward. Shock stumbled away with a great sword cut across his belly. That wound alone would have finished him in time, but the valiant brute swung around blindly, hungering for one good grip of his jaws on the enemy.

He might as well have gripped at a ghost. Frosty side-stepped, then bowled Shock over and put his grip on the throat.

When he stood back, Shock lay still, and there was a vague comfort in the heart of the wolf.

He knew, if ever an animal could have known, that battle was his destiny, and then death in the wild. Now he had fought, and the dead lay around him. No matter what happened then, even with this single day behind him, he had not lived in vain.

It was then that he heard the heavy, clumsy beat of the foot of man, for big Bill Gary was approaching swiftly. By the footfall alone, Frosty would have known that it was man. He did not need the scent of powder and steel that was blowing down the wind to him. He knew now that he had no time even to sever his leg below the trap and go halting away. In all the world of his cunning devices there was only one poor expedient left, and that was to drop and lie like a stone.

He had seen other animals play possum, but none ever played it better than Frosty as he lay with glassy eyes partly open, his mouth wide, his tongue lolling out on the pine needles. His very breathing was so controlled that only the most considerate eye could have detected the rise and fall of his ribs beneath their deep coating of fur.

That was the picture that Bill Gary saw as he came rushing out into the clearing. He saw Shock dead, Tiger kicking himself around in the last struggle for breath, a big wolf also dead, with one leg caught in a trap, and above all—a sight that made all else as nothing in his mind —here was, at last, the great marauder, Frosty, stretched on the ground with open mouth and tongue lolling!

They had killed Frosty, and he had taken toll of his slayers. Well, it was a pity to lose Shock and Tiger, but, after all, one has to pay for great results. People would remember him for this. They would say, in days to come: "Bill Gary, that rich man—that fellow that found the great gold mine—the same one that caught Frosty, the famous wolf."

That was the way people would have to talk about him. Because it is possible to overlook a man who has done only one thing—the accomplishment may be put down to luck or to chance—but when a man has done two outstanding things, his peers must stand back and take off their hats.

The battle was plainly over. So the trapper put his rifle against a tree and came forward with only the ax in his hand. He came on slowly, with the loss of his two fine dogs a diminishing fact in his mind, every instant, and glory in the taking of Frosty outruling all other things in the world. It grew in his passionate mind into a thing equal with the finding of the gold mine. If he had had to take his choice between the two accomplishments at that instant, perhaps he would have preferred the trapping of the great wolf.

He was a monster. Bill Gary had sometimes felt that the size of the footprint could not really have indicated the actual bulk of the marauder. He called Frosty, in his own mind, "Big-foot." And yet here was the actuality spread magnificently over the ground. There was no other wolf in the world like this, he was sure. Two thousand dollars? It no longer seemed an absurdly high reward for the catching of the monster. It was almost worth two thousand dollars to have one look at that king of the wilderness and see what a wolf could really be like!

Those were the thoughts of big Bill Gary as he strolled up closer and closer to the spot where the wolf lay, with the wind ruffling his fur. He came within three steps, within two, within one.

And then the heap of fur twitched into life. Bill Gary had a chance to heave up the ax, but he was far too late to spring back. The slash of the knife-sharp fangs caught him across the inside of his right thigh and cut through the tough cloth of his trousers, and into the deep, soft flesh—cutting and tearing.

27

The wrenching force of that stroke dropped big Bill Gary to his knees. The agony of the torn flesh half blinded his eyes. It was a smoke of pain filled with red sparks that flared up across his mind, and through it he saw Frosty.

He struck at the leaping form. The blow of the ax glanced, and the teeth of the wolf reached at his throat. He struck with all the force of his left hand. The blow fell; the teeth ripped all the tendons inside his wrist with a knife stroke.

He had only one hand, now, for the swaying of the ax, and Frosty, with blood-dripping mouth, was rushing in at him again.

He had the ax by the narrow neck as he struck to parry that rush. The wolf swerved from the blow and came in again, and with a half swing of his arm, Bill Gary smashed the back of the ax home right on the broad top of Frosty's head.

The lobo dropped, either stunned or brained. But, impelled by the force of his leap, he struck against the legs of Gary. The breath went out of Frosty's body with an audible grunt. The impact knocked Gary backward, and as he strove to get to his feet, his wounded right leg gave way under him, and he fell on his side.

A mist of whirling darkness poured over his brain, and he fainted.

CHAPTER V

Freedom for Frosty

THE total surprise, the horror of the grinning mask of the wolf, the agony of the wounds, the hot gushing of his own blood, had unstrung even the steel nerves of Bill Gary— but only for a few moments.

When he recovered and sat up, he was lying in a pool of blood. And more blood was pumping out of his thigh and out of his wrist. Arteries had been severed in both places —big arteries.

He knew the extent of the danger by the frightful giddiness of his brain. There was still strength in one hand, however. As for the left hand, he would never be able to use that again. Or would the cunning doctors actually be able to tie severed tendons together?

To stop the blood was the first thing.

He knew that those few moments of unconsciousness during which he had lain on the ground had brought him to the verge of death, for his heart had been strongly pumping out his lifeblood every instant of that time.

Now, in a frenzy of panic, he wanted to stop both flows of blood at once.

He steadied himself. He could not do both things at once. That was impossible. It was a time to make every second count, to be calm and cool. So he made himself calm and cool.

He ripped off his coat with his right hand.

He kneeled on the coat, held one edge of it between his teeth, and with his hunting knife slashed off several strips. He took two of those strips, still working with teeth and hand, and twisted them together. The gaping wound in his thigh was what counted most. He ran the cloth around the top of his leg and knotted it. It was barely long enough to serve the purpose. He had to lean over and almost break his back, to catch one end of the cloth in his teeth. Then he worked the bandage up. He took a short stick, shoved it inside the bandage, and twisted.

As he twisted, he saw the compression of the flesh open the gaping mouth of the wound, but the flow of the blood diminished. He kept on twisting until the bandage pressed down through his flesh. The agony of it burned him to the bone. But he kept on until not a drop of blood was flowing from the wound. Then he took out a bit of twine—what man of the wilds will do without string or thongs of some sort in his pockets—and lashed the stick in place.

After that, he did the same thing with his torn wrist. The devil was in the wolf that it had been able to open arteries with each stroke of its fangs! The devil was in the wolf, and in the luck of Bill Gary.

Then he told himself that this was his payment. He had found incredible wealth. He had unlocked the ribs of the ancient mountains to get at it. Well, there is always bad luck in store for the finders of treasure. He was having his misfortune now.

Afterward, in the long years to come, he would be able to revel in the wealth. He would be able to look back on the day when he had fought with that incarnate fiend, Frosty.

Who in the world had ever heard of a wolf playing possum before? Yes, they had been known to do it. Coyotes will do it, too.

Then, as he finally sealed up the flow of blood on his

wrists, he became very faint, and was nauseated. The trees spun around and around before his eyes.

He endured that, closing his eyes, stretching himself on his back. He was almost glad of the two hot bands of agony that were biting into his flesh on his leg and on his arm. That pain would bring him back to his senses. Or had he already lost so much blood that he was sure to die?

He put a hand over his heart and could feel nothing. He listened calmly, and made out by sense, not by sound, the fluttering pulsation.

Live? Of course he would live! He pushed himself to a sitting posture. His left arm was blackening and swelling with the checked currents of the blood. His leg below the bandage was numb. Half of him was dead already. He felt that. He was suddenly, calmly sure that he would in fact die before he ever managed to get back to the cabin.

If he got back to the cabin, he could light two fires in front of his shack. That smoke, as it rose, would be a signal to Luke Warner, three miles farther down the valley. He and Luke had arranged the signals long before. A man may get terribly ill or may have an accident which keeps him from traveling through the mountains. In case anything happened to one of them, they were to send the signal—two columns of smoke, steadily rising.

If he could get back to the cabin, he could manage to light the fires, and then Luke Warner would come: Luke was a fellow to be depended upon. Mean and hard, but dependable.

The nausea returned upon him. Something was sickening him, and he told himself that it was the smell of wolf.

That made him look at the motionless body of the great lobo, and he saw that from the place where the ragged back of the ax had torn the scalp of the wolf, blood was flowing. Well, blood does not flow from dead bodies, and, therefore, Frosty was still alive!

The mouth of Bill Gary twisted to the side. It was almost a smile. There was a chance—one chance in ten thousand—that some one might come up here and find the two dogs, the other wolf, and Gary himself lying dead —and Frosty still alive!

31

That lucky stranger would claim the scalp money! He would get the bounty that really belonged to a dead man!

And suddenly Bill Gary hated the entire living world of man. They lived, and little did they care how he lay in agony on the mountain, slowly dying!

They lived, and the wolf lived.

He crawled over to the tree. It was hard to hunch himself along on one knee and one hand. He put his ruined left hand down and used the left arm, also. The agony was only a little more frightful. What bothered him most was the thought of the pine needles and the dirt getting into the opening and shutting wound in his wrist.

He got the rifle, tied it to him, and crawled back to shoot Frosty. The blood was still trickling from the head of the stunned wolf.

Then another thought came to him.

If he died, and the wolf died, then his gold mine was lost. No man would ever find it, because these mountains had been prospected thoroughly for gold and the miners had given up. The secret of the mine would be lost. In a single year or so the weather would cover over the raw wounds in the ledge where the gleam of the gold still shone out.

The greatest thing in his life would then be as nothing! It would be almost as though he had not lived, in fact!

When he thought of that, he cursed softly. If he used too much breath, it started him gasping, and the trees and the mountains spun around him in dark, swift circles.

That was when he remembered the Red Cross collars on the dead dogs, and with a stroke of imagination his mind leaped the rest of the way. He went to Shock, the nearest body, and unbuckled the heavy steel collar. He took out his notebook, opened it, and wrote with his indelible pencil, under his last entry:

DEAR ALEC: Go to place described and find a ledge with a gold outcrop. I think I'm dying. Good luck to you. I give you the mine. It's as rich as thunder.

BILL GARY.

He tore the page out of the book and folded it small. On the outside, he wrote the address: "Alexander Gary, Newlands. Please deliver."

He wrapped that folded bit of paper in some of the oiled silk, opened the little compartment in the dog collar, and placed the message inside. Then he crawled to the senseless body of the wolf and fastened the collar around the great neck. It fitted so snugly that he could be sure the beast would not be able to rub it off.

Watching closely, he could see the slight rise and fall of the ribs as the senseless monster breathed. He was glad. He was wonderfully glad that his messenger might live— if only the ax stroke had not shattered the skull.

He crawled to the rear leg that was fastened in the trap. He had to bear down with his ruined left hand and with his right to unspring the powerful trap. And his head spun around as he made the effort.

But at last the great wolf was free.

Bill Gary dragged himself to a little distance and got his back to a tree.

To lie down and die, like a silly fool, like a baby—that would be too horrible for speech. But to die sitting up, looking the world in the face—that was not so bad.

He wanted to see the wolf get up and start away before he gave up the ghost.

Then he remembered that he had a small metal flask of whisky in his hip pocket. It shocked him to think that he could have forgotten this until such a late moment. Instantly the flask was uncorked and half the contents flowed down his throat.

When he looked up from his drink, he saw Frosty actually rising to his feet. He swayed a moment, staggered, and then, with a motion as fluidly sliding as though there were not a wound on his body, Frosty faded away among the trees and was gone.

He was gone, but he could not escape men forever. He had learned much wisdom in his life. No doubt this one day had taught him several profound chapters. But nevertheless he could not hold out forever against the wiles of traps, poison, hunting packs of fast and savage dogs and, above all, high-power rifles. Some day he would fall. And when he fell, certainly the mystery of finding a steel collar around his throat would cause the collar to be removed. Might it start merely a legend that Frosty was not a wolf at all, but merely a dog that had run wild?

But surely, one day, men would open the little container and find therein the message.

So Gary's great enemy, Frosty, became his one link with the world, the hand which he reached out for the recognition of posterity.

For when the message was read, the mine would be discovered, and then—well, they could hardly do less than name the mine after him. For every drop of blood shed from his veins, an ounce of yellow gold would pour out into circulation. It would work evil and it would work good, here and there. And all that it accomplished would be the work of a dead man, Bill Gary.

It was a satisfaction to him. It was a foretaste of immortality. It made him smile.

And, above all, it seemed to Bill Gary most right and fitting that he should have fastened his gift to the world around the neck of a wolf.

CHAPTER VI

The Fugitives

AFTER a while big Bill Gary stopped meditating about death because he was tired of it, and because a cold wind began to thrill through his wounds. Their pain had joined. The pain from the wrist rose up the arm and at the shoulder it encountered the pain from the wounded thigh, which possessed all the rest of the body.

Bill Gary was tired of sitting there. If it were better to meet death sitting down than lying down, it was still better to meet death in action than in repose, so he began to act.

He crawled out of the clearing, out of the strip of trees, and to the verge of the treeless waste of snow. He was a mile above the cabin, and he started for it, not because he thought that he had strength to get there, but because he despised inactive waiting for the end.

It was easier than he expected. It was the sort of a thing that one can do more easily than think. To crawl a mile would have been totally impossible, and he could not have gone a hundred yards up a slope, but this was different. He had snow under him all the way, and there was a continually declining slope to the ground. He could half roll and half slide. He moved his body like a fish wriggling through slime rather than like a land animal. He received a heavy battering before he got to the bottom of the rise among the trees that shrouded his shack. He half rolled and half crawled to the cabin, and fainted on the threshold of it.

When he wakened again, a few minutes later, he found himself much weaker. There was a hurrying pulse in his temples like a clock ticking all out of time. Everything that his eyes looked on shuddered as though an earthquake were shaking the ground.

He said to himself: "Bill, you're going to die, you old fool!"

Then he thought of the mine again, and he was sorry that he had inclosed the news of it in the collar of the wolf. If he had only known that he could reach his cabin, he would have waited and written a letter. Then, with his pair of smokes, he could have called up Warner and confided the letter to him to be mailed, a month or so later, when Warner went to town.

He would still be able to write the letter, he told himself. He was going to die, all right, but not immediately. There was the sort of metal in him that rubs out only after long and constant friction.

He dragged himself to his knees and got to the table of soft pine, which he had made himself. He had built a drawer under that table. He was prouder of that drawer than of almost anything he had ever done, because it was a homemade luxury such as most men of the wilderness would not have considered worthy of thought. It was this drawer that he drew open, and then he worked himself up onto the bench that ranged beside the table.

Then he lay across the table for a moment, nauseated more than ever, his brain whirling. He wished that he could die without being sick at the stomach.

He pushed himself erect. The top of the table was new and white because it was only recently made, and planed down. Now there was blood on it. In his rolling, sliding descent, his clothes had been caught and torn in many

36

places; his flesh had been caught and torn, also. The blood stood out on the top of the table as on a field of snow.

He got out of the drawer a sheet of letter paper and an envelope. In indelible pencil he wrote the address first:

MR. ALEXANDER GARY,
    Newlands.

Then he started on the sheet of paper:

DEAR ALEC: I'm done for. I got Frosty, and Frosty got me.

I've tapped open the biggest vein of gold, to-day, that you ever seen. Then I caught Frosty in a trap, and he chawed me almost to death.

I took and wrote out the description of where to find the mine and put one of my dogs' Red Cross collars on Frosty and put the description in the collar and turned Frosty loose, because I thought that I sure never would—

His hand paused.

It was hard work pushing the pencil, because it bit not only into the paper, but also into the softness of the wood on which the paper smoothly rested.

There was a cloud before his eyes. This time it was not whirling, but it was thickening and moving up on him, little by little. He rubbed the back of his hand across his eyes, but that did not help very much. The darkness kept on growing.

He got out the flask of whisky.

"Hell," said Bill Gary, "it's like as though there was a kind of a night in the middle of the day."

He could not uncork the flask with his numb fingers, but he worried it out with his teeth. He drank the rest of what was in the flask, holding the neck of the bottle between his teeth. It slewed out of his mouth, when it was emptied, and bumped on his shoulder on the way to the floor.

He was no longer nauseated, and he was glad of that. He told himself that perhaps he would not die. He wanted

37

to go to sleep for a minute, and after that, he would wake up and finish writing the letter. Alec Gary was a good kid, and Alec ought to have the mine—if Bill Gary died.

Bill Gary put his forehead on his right arm. Everything was confused, and red lights began to move in his darkness, not whirling about, but wavering toward him like lanterns swinging at the sides of walking men. He closed his eyes harder. The darkness grew complete. He slept.

That was the way Barry Christian and Duff Gregor found him. It is hard to say that blind chance brought Barry Christian, the greatest of all criminal brains and hands, through the mountains at exactly the right time to find Bill Gary dead with the news of the finding of the gold mine written out on a piece of paper. It is easier and more convenient to say that there was a malice in Fate which had designed this happening with malignant care.

For many miles now, Barry Christian and Duff Gregor had been fleeing. They had had almost a dozen men about them in the beginning; they had only themselves now. For Jim Silver had hounded them closely all the way. He was still hounding them, perhaps, unless the strength had finally departed out of the tireless limbs of Parade, the golden stallion.

A great, bright ghost, Parade had stridden over the leagues behind them. All the others among the pursuers, gradually, had dropped away. All the others of the fugitives had been worn out and turned to this side or to that.

Only Barry Christian kept on, with Duff Gregor. Gregor himself, big and strong as he was, would have fallen away with the rest, except that Christian gave him extra support and help, the reason being that the resemblance of Gregor to Jim Silver had been helpful to Barry before and might prove helpful again. So Christian kept him along.

They had worn out one set of horses after another. Where they could buy horses, they bought them. Where they could not buy horses, they stole them. They crossed the Bull's Head Range on foot, a hundred terrible miles that Christian forced Duff Gregor to travel. He walked behind Gregor.

The last twenty miles, he beat Gregor like a beast, with

his quirt. When Gregor fell from exhaustion, Barry Christian kicked him to his feet again and forced him to travel on.

They got horses on the other side of the range. Christian tied Duff Gregor into the saddle and led the horse ahead, while Gregor lay senseless with sleep. That was the way they had managed to keep out of the grasp of Jim Silver on Parade. That was the only way.

It might be that on the edge of the Blue Waters they had shaken the great Silver off the trail. It was more likely that Silver was somewhere behind them, either reading their sign or else guessing with his accustomed uncanny accuracy what was going on inside their minds. Duff Gregor, for his part, felt that death itself was almost better than being pursued any longer in this fashion. The pain of death could bite him to the bone only once, whereas now he was dying every day of his life, a hundred times over.

The big body of Duff Gregor looked more like that of Jim Silver than ever before, for the immense labor of the flight had taken away all excess flesh and left him with his shoulders broad and heavy and the rest of the body tapering off.

His face looked more like the face of Silver than ever, also. It, too, had been refined by agony. Only his forehead was different, for the brow of Silver always held a sort of gloomy serenity, and the brow of Duff Gregor was heavily contracted.

As they came up the hillside, this day, it was Gregor who first noticed the hint of a trail and said:

"Somebody lives not far from here."

"We'll find 'em all right," said Christian.

"So that we can leave our trail posted for Silver?" asked Gregor satirically.

The pale, handsome face of Barry Christian turned toward his companion, and he smiled. His gentle and musical voice answered: "We need fresh horses, partner."

"Not likely to be horses, where we're heading. This isn't a horse trail, you can see."

"This isn't a horse trail, but there may be horses, and

if there are not horses, there may be burros. Anything will be useful. Even a dog."

"You mean," said Duff Gregor, looking about the tips of the trees at the blue-white of the sea above timber line that extended into the sky, "you mean that you're really going to cross the Blue Waters in one march?"

"Not in one march," said Christian. "We'll camp for one night up yonder, and freeze and chatter our teeth till the morning. And then we'll go on again and try to finish the crossing to-morrow."

"I'd rather turn around and face Jim Silver," cried out Duff Gregor, in a passion. "I'd rather face him and have it out with him. Look! We're two men, and he's only one!"

Barry Christian looked not at Gregor, but down at his long, graceful hands.

Many a man said, and was willing to swear to it, that those famous hands of Barry Christian were even more dreadful with weapons than were the hands of Jim Silver. Even if they were not, there could not be very much actual difference between the prowess of the two men.

"You can beat him all by yourself, Barry!" cried Duff Gregor. "You can beat anybody in the world, if you make up your mind to it."

Barry Christian slowly shook his head. Sorrow came into his face and made it handsomer than ever—like the face of one suffering spiritual pain beyond the concerns of this earth of ours.

"Silver's beaten me," he said. "He's beaten me with his bare hands and he's beaten me with guns. He's outtricked and he's outfought me. Sometimes I even think that the only reason I'm permitted to be alive is so that the young men of the world can have the spectacle of Barry Christian being kicked around the world by the great Jim Silver, the upholder of the law. That's a moral sight. Deters the youth of the country from crime."

Duff Gregor suddenly grinned. When he smiled, all the brute in him came out, and his entire resemblance to Jim Silver flickered and then went out.

"By thunder, Barry," he said, "when I hear you talk

like that, it's as good as reading a book. You say the queerest things!"

"Do I?" asked Christian softly.

No one could tell what he meant, when he looked and spoke like this. Sometimes Duff Gregor half expected to have his throat cut and be left by the trail. That would be the instant that Christian decided that Gregor was more of a present encumbrance than a future assistance. In any case, he would not want Gregor to fall alive into the hands of his enemies. Gregor knew too much.

"Perhaps you're right," said Christian. "Perhaps I should have been a teacher or a minister, or some such thing, leading a secluded life, and trying to help other men toward a vision of the truth."

Big Duff Gregor filled the woods with his bawling laughter.

"There you go again. You sure beat me. You beat anybody. You're a scream, Barry! Hey, there's the house!"

Through the tree trunks they saw the broken picture of the little house. Falling snow obscured it, also. The sky was filled with deep miles of gray that promised a soft ocean of snow to descend upon the earth.

CHAPTER VII

Outlaw's Plan

CHRISTAIN went in first. He was always first, when Gregor was his companion, because he profoundly distrusted everything that Gregor was apt to do in an emergency. He detested Gregor with all his soul, as he would have detested a false coin. But still, the resemblance between the man and the famous Jim Silver was too great to permit him to be discarded. Counterfeit he was, but even so he might be of immense use in the future.

At the door of the shack, Christian saw the great body of Bill Gary spilled across the table. He called, got no answer, and stepped to the table. His head was still bent above the still figure when Gregor asked calmly: "That mug is dead, isn't he?"

Christian slowly lifted his head and looked toward Gregor.

"Yes, he's dead."

Big Gregor stepped to the table and stared calmly down at the body. He had seen plenty of death—since he had joined the forces of Barry Christian.

"Look at— His left wrist is all torn."

"I see it," said Barry Christian.

He picked up the loose weight of Bill Gary, grasping him under the armpits, and dragged him toward the bunk that was built against the wall. A paper fluttered from the top of the table to the floor.

Gregor picked up the feet of the dead man and helped lay him on the bunk.

"Torn all to the devil," said Gregor.

"Something got at him. Dogs—wolves," said Christian. He looked around the shack at the extra traps. "A trapper, and the wolves got him. That's rather pretty."

"Yeah, that's pretty," said Gregor.

He picked up the fallen paper. Christian was pulling a blanket over the face of the dead man, and, turning, he asked:

"What was that?"

"That? What?" asked Gregor.

"That thing you picked up."

"Oh, nothing."

"You certainly wouldn't pick up nothing."

"What could a gent pick up in a place like this?"

"There was a piece of paper."

"Yeah. With some stuff scribbled over it," said Gregor.

"Let's see it."

"Ain't worth seeing."

Christian held out his left hand. Their eyes met, and those of Gregor fell away.

"All right," he said. "Just a crazy idea out of a dead man's head."

"Dead men tell the truth, if they talk at all," said Christian.

He took the paper which Gregor had crumpled, thrusting it into his pocket. Christian spread it out and read the contents aloud.

DEAR ALEC: I'm done for. I got Frosty, and Frosty got me.

I've tapped open the biggest vein of gold, to-day, that you ever seen. Then I caught Frosty in a trap, and he chawed me almost to death.

He paused and looked at Gregor. Gregor hung his head.

"I thought it was just a crazy lot of drool," said Gregor.

Christian said nothing. He continued to hold Gregor with his eye, like a fish dangling, dying at the end of a line. Then he went on with the remaining few lines, reading them aloud, quietly.

He lowered the paper and then he said:

"Nerve. That's what that dead man had. He traveled quite a distance on that ruined hand and spoiled leg. He crawled and rolled and slid. See how his clothes were torn to pieces?"

"Yeah, I seen," said Gregor. "Think that there's anything in that drool?"

"You know there's something in it," answered Christian. "You're dead certain that there's something in it. Otherwise, you wouldn't have planned to hold out the paper, duck away from me, and finally come back to this part of the world and look up Frosty."

"Hey, listen, Barry—" began Gregor in a pleading voice.

Christian bit his lip as though to keep it from curling with contempt.

"I understand," he said. "I know you pretty well, Gregor. But I hoped that I didn't know you as well as all this."

"You take it pretty hard," said Gregor, "when all I meant was—"

"Quit it," said Christian.

Gregor was gloomily silent.

Barry Christian picked up the envelope.

"This letter ought to go," he said, "to the hands of one Alexander Gary, in the town of Newlands. Unfortunately for him, however, he'll never see it. The letter has come into better hands than his, and those hands will find the gold mine, I imagine."

"It's a dog-gone queer thing," muttered Gregor. "I never heard of anything like it."

"Neither have I," said Christian.

He stared with narrowed eyes at his companion.

"It means several things," he said. "One is, that you're going to have your wish, Gregor."

"What wish?" asked Gregor, half frightened by the tone and the cold, calm manner of Christian.

"It means," said Christian, "that we're going to run no longer. We're going to stand our ground, and if Jim Silver overtakes us, we're going to fight it out with him. Does that suit you?"

Gregor closed his eyes and shuddered. Then, looking up again, he muttered:

"We were running for our lives a minute ago. There wasn't hardly anything to live for. But, now we've as good as got a gold mine, things look different, Barry. Why should we go and chuck ourselves away on a fight with Jim Silver, just for the fun of it?"

He waited with a puckered brow, as one who is reasonably sure of receiving a reproof, but the pale, handsome face of Christian merely smiled in return.

"I can understand that state of mind, too," he answered. "After all, Gregor, it's a pleasure to be with you. Whatever you do, you'll never surprise me. It's like listening to a twice-told tale. Well, here we are in the Blue Water Mountains, and here we stay until we find the wolf called Frosty. And on the neck of Frosty there's an iron collar, and somewhere in that collar there is the description of the location of the vein of gold. Is that clear?"

"That's clear," muttered Gregor. "Sure it is."

He added: "And Jim Silver?"

"Jim Silver," said Christian, "may have had enough hunting to suit even him. He's followed this trail until even his best friend, Taxi, was worn out and had to quit the job. And Taxi has the strength and the endurance of a wild beast, when it comes to following a blood trail. It may be that Jim Silver is not following us into these mountains. If he *is* following us, he expects us to try to cut straight across the summits."

"Through a storm like this?" queried Gregor.

"He knows that we've gone through worse than this, to get away from him," said Christian. "He knows that we've gone through hot hell and cold hell to get away from him, and a little feathery snowstorm like this could never stop us, I imagine he'll think. No, he'll drive straight through the mountains, and try to catch us on the other side."

"And we?" asked Gregor hopefully. "We camp here?"

"Camp here?" asked Christian, lifting his brows with a touch of surprise. "Are you out of your head, Gregor? Stay here in this shack as if we were in a trap, in case he manages to come up with the place? That would be pretty convenient for Jim Silver, Gregor. That would be about all that he would ask out of life—to find the pair of us lodged together in one house!"

Gregor nodded.

"Well, then," he said, "you tell us what we're to do. We go on with these horses, and they freeze in the cold unless they keep traveling, and then—"

Christian raised a hand, and the other was silent.

"We have to do a little inquiring," he said. "It's as plain as can be that this dead man was a wolf trapper. It's as plain as can be that he trapped a wolf and the wolf chewed him up. We'll have to ask some one what that wolf was like."

Gregor stared helplessly.

"You ain't gone crazy, Barry, have you?" he asked.

"I don't think so."

"But look here. Who would know what that wolf is like? All wolves are about the same! Who could know what the wolf was like?"

"Because," said Christian, "he has a name—Frosty. And that means that he's a celebrity. One wolf in a million raises enough devil to get a nickname from people. You'll find that every man in these mountains knows something about Frosty, I suppose."

CHAPTER VIII

The Pursuer

BLUE-GRAY dusk settled down through the blackness of the trees. The falling snow pressed the evening close on the heads of the pines. In the great smother of the storm the wind whirled, above the forest, and made obscure pools of motion. It was very cold; it was growing momentarily colder, for the wind came off the higher peaks to the northwest.

But Jim Silver kept Parade to his work.

He had lost all sign of the two men he was trailing something over an hour before. He could only hope, as he had hoped so often before, that he had been able to read the minds of the fugitives, and that he could guess in what direction they were riding. He felt, on the whole, that the pair would try to cut straight across the Blue Water Mountains in a couple of marches.

He must follow. He felt that it would be best to strike right across to the farther side, not trying to find trail on the way, and then, in the distance, attempt to pick up the sign again. It would be very hard on Parade to make that forced march, but the stallion was whalebone and finest spring steel, and he would not fail.

This very night, they would have to camp far above timber line, in the lee of some bluff; else they would have to move slowly on, all during the night.

Silver swung down from the saddle and ran ahead, throwing the lines of the hackamore over the pommel of the saddle and leaving the stallion to follow.

In this manner he gained two advantages. One was that he took his weight off the back of the horse. The other was that he broke trail for the stallion, to a certain extent, for he could depend on Parade to step exactly where his master had trod before him.

As for the burning up of Silver's own strength, that did not matter. Nothing mattered except the horse. And it was this attitude of his, relentlessly enforced by practice all the way, that had enabled him to keep so close to the heels of men who were constantly picking up fresh relays of horse-flesh to carry them away. Of the hundreds of miles they had traveled since the chase began—that great chase which men were never to forget—a good third of the distance had been covered by Silver on foot, with Parade following easily behind, like a dog at the heels of his master.

In rough going, of steep ups and downs, Silver actually was on foot more than he was in the saddle. He had divorced himself utterly from the usual Western viewpoint, that man is helpless on his feet and must have a saddle to hold his weight. Like an Indian, patiently, Silver was accustomed to traveling over rough or smooth until exhaustion made his head swim. Then, and only then, he gave his weight to the saddle again.

So it was that he ran down the near slope and then plodded steadily up the farther one with the head of the great horse nodding behind him. He used his eyes little, because the light was much too dim for them to be of much service. It was true that Christian and Gregor might at any moment have decided to turn back and waylay their enemy, but in that case he would trust to the wolfish keenness of the scent of Parade. The nostrils of Parade retained the wisdom they had picked up during the years when he had wandered as a wild horse through the mountain desert. And at the first suspicious sound or scent, he would give warning to his human companion.

By night, also, it was better to have Parade at hand than any pair of human sentinels, no matter how keen of vision and hearing. There was a perfect partnership between the two. One was complementary to the other. Each had a perfect trust.

Silver was well up the hillside before he came out of the trees into a little clearing at the very instant when the snort and stamp of Parade warned him that there might be danger ahead. And now, vaguely outlined through the falling snow of the twilight, Silver saw the silhouette of the shack.

He held up his hand in a gesture which would force Parade to remain in place. Then he stole forward cautiously.

The shack was probably uninhabited. Otherwise it would almost surely be lighted by a fire at this time of the day; since it was not likely that its occupant might be off on a trip in such weather as this. The greatest likelihood was that it had been thrown up by some prospector or trapper, and was long since abandoned.

And yet no cautious wolf could have investigated the probable lair of a mountain lion with more care than Jim Silver showed as he advanced toward the place.

He circled to the rear of it, first of all, and brought himself close to the wall, where he crouched, listening intently, shutting the noise of the storm out of his mind, and concentrating on any sound that might come out of the interior.

He heard nothing, except those mysterious breathings which the wind makes through imperfect walls.

After a time, he went to the front of the place, and found the door. It was latched, but not locked. There was a latchstring which he used, and then pushed the door open with a swift gesture and stepped inside.

The thickness of the darkness was now perfect. And around him he found the odor of cookery which was not of a very ancient date. The fumes of fried bacon will linger for a long time on the walls of a shack.

There was the smell of cookery, which proved that the shack was inhabited, or at least that it had been used not long before. That made it doubly strange to find the place empty and dark.

He felt down the wall until his hand touched a lantern. That he took off its peg, raised the chimney, and lighted the wick. Even then he was so uneasy that he made a long stride back from the light.

What he saw first was the shining white surface of the pine table on which he had placed the lantern. Next he was aware of the crazy little cast-iron stove, in the corner, with a rusted length of stovepipe rising above it through the roof. There were old traps piled in several places. There were battered clothes hanging along the wall. A saddle hung from a peg, a pack saddle from another. And on a bunk in a corner of the room was a man stretched out with a blanket pulled over his head, sleeping so hard, apparently, that even the noise of the lighting of the lan-- tern had not wakened him.

"Hello!" called Silver.

Then an icy finger ran down his spine.

He stepped to the bunk and gradually drew the blanket away from an unshaven, shaggy face. The eyes of the man were partially open. There was a faint, derisive smile on his lips.

It seemed, as Silver drew the blanket completely away, that the smile of derision was directed toward the sleeper's own body, for the clothes were torn to rags on it, the left arm was frightfully gashed at the wrist, and there was a powerful tourniquet above the wound.

The right thigh was badly mangled on the inside of the leg, also, and there was another tourniquet above that injury.

The right hand lay on the chest. Silver touched it, and found it as hard and as cold as a stone. This sleeper would never waken again.

He went back to the table. By the bloodstains he saw how the wounded man had slumped across it. A pencil lay on the earthen floor, which was marked by the imprint of small heels, like those of the boots of a cowpuncher, far different from the big shoes of the dead man. There were two sets of those imprints; therefore two men had been there. They had carried the burden to the bunk. Yes, for here were the deeper signs to indicate how they had lifted and bórne the weight. They had stretched him on the bunk and covered his face. Then they had gone away. Two men—Barry Christian and Duff Gregor, perhaps. By the sizes of the footmarks, it could hardly have been any others who had visited here.

Jim Silver turned hastily to the door to remount Parade and push ahead through the storm. He was about to extinguish the lantern when he thought of the dead man again, and paused.

No matter how keen he was to pursue the trail, he could not leave the body to decay, unheeded. It might be years before another traveler penetrated to this obscure corner of the mountains.

He carried the lantern outside. The snow was still falling rapidly, and through the dim pencilings that it made in the air, he saw a perfect place for a grave, a natural hollow in the side of the slope, with plenty of loose rock about it.

He went back into the cabin, swathed the body in the blanket, and carried the rigid form outside. In the hollow he laid it with a decent gravity. He picked up a handful of gravel and let it fall gradually on the corpse.

"Whoever you may be," said Jim Silver, taking his sombrero from his head, "good hunting!"

He began to push in the large rocks. Under a yard of heavy stones he buried the stranger. Then he went inside the cabin to put out the lantern and leave it. As he put the lantern on the table, however, he noticed a portion of a side of bacon hanging in the corner near the stove, tied up by a bit of twine, as though to keep it from rats. And the sight of this puzzled him greatly. For he had every reason to think that Gregor and Christian were hungry travelers. He had pushed them hard. It was long since they had had a chance to lay in new supplies of food, and yet they had overlooked this invaluable meat! Neither were they fellows who would spare the goods of a dead man!

Deep in thought, he tapped his fingers on the white, shining surface of the table. It could not have been his coming that had frightened the pair away. They could not have seen him approaching. Something must have drawn their minds away from the thought of eating. But what is stronger in the mind of a hungry man than the desire for food?

He considered the red stains on the table, the pencil on the floor. He picked it up. It was indelible, with a very hard lead. The table drawer was partly ajar, and there was writing paper in it. It seemed plain that the dead man had been found slumped forward on the table, writing.

And that was strangest of all! For why should a man on the verge of death, so horribly torn by wolves or dogs, have sat down to spend his last moments writing? To a wife? Well, the haggard, savage face of the corpse had not been that of a sentimentalist.

Silver sat down at the table and leaned his own body above the red stains. The sensitive tips of his fingers, at the same time, slipped over impressions which had been faintly grooved in the soft surface of the wood. He put his eye almost on a level with the table top, and now he saw the dim impression of writing which had registered through the paper on the tender pine.

He went to the stove, got a bit of a charred ember of wood, and delicately drew it back and forth over the writing, until the depressions stood out as lines of white in the midst of the black shading. Letters, words, appeared, some dim, but all legible, and the opening phrases were enough to make his blood leap:

DEAR ALEC: I'm done for. I got Frosty, and Frosty got me.

I've tapped open the biggest vein of gold, to-day, that you ever seen.

CHAPTER IX

Alec Gary

THERE was one bit of testimony which was important to Jim Silver, and that was an envelope which had been carelessly crumpled in the hand and thrown behind the stove. The address on it was "Alexander Gary, Newlands." That name, since it was put down in the handwriting that had appeared upon the surface of the table, and since the "Dear Alec" of the table inscription suited the name on the envelope, convinced Jim Silver that he had found the man to whom the dead man had determined to make over the claim which he had discovered.

It left Silver in a quandary.

He had no doubt, now, that the great Barry Christian and his companion, Duff Gregor, were somewhere in the mountains trying to get their hands—or their guns—on a wolf sufficiently famous to have won a nickname among men. And if they succeeded, Christian would find, in a collar which had been strangely placed upon the neck of the animal by human hands, the secret of the claim's location.

In the meantime, in the town of Newlands, wherever

that might be, was to be found the fellow to whom the dying man had willed his discovery.

The great problem of Silver was to get at Christian. Now he had help on the trail, because if he could find Frosty, the wolf, he would probably find Barry Christian not far off. The two things worked together. And the only complication was the existence of this man Alexander Gary.

It was no great pinching of the heart of Jim Silver to give up all hope of getting any of the gold for himself. It was not the first time that he had turned his back on fortune. Neither would it be the last. And besides, he was fascinated by the thought of that savage-faced wolf hunter, the dead man, who had sent abroad the message of his discovery tied to the neck of a wild wolf, and who, with the last of his strength, had striven to send word to this Alexander Gary, also.

That was why Jim Silver left the upper Blue Waters and went to the little town of Newlands, on the edge of the range.

In the town he learned that Alec Gary had an uncle, Bill Gary, who was well known as a ruffian and a wolf hunter. Alec Gary had, also, a job on the Chester ranch, not far from the town. The postmaster readily told him that, and Silver slipped out of the town, unobserved.

He was lucky in doing so, he felt, for during recent days more and more men knew that the rider of a great chestnut stallion *might* be Jim Silver. And when they knew the name, they knew everything else. They knew all the long story of his exploits, and that meant public applause, questions, and a surrounding atmosphere of awe which always pinched the heart of Silver and made him wish, more than ever, for the quiet of the wilderness.

He used to tell himself, over and over again, that the trail of Barry Christian was the last one that he would pursue. Once that was completed, Jim Silver would retire forever into the still peace of the mountains and live forever alone.

He thought this more than ever on this day, as he rode out of Newlands toward the Chester ranch. He took off his sombrero and let the wind blow through his hair. At other times he dared not expose his head, if men were around, for fear that even the most casual eye would not fail to notice the two tufts of gray hair above his temples, like incipient horns beginning to thrust out. They knew his face, too often, as well. His picture had got into the newspapers, into the magazines. Some fool had written a life of him and told everything wrong, and gilded him brighter than gold. He had managed to wade far enough into the reading of that book to be bogged down with the lies that were told.

In fact, he knew that he had become, in spite of himself, a public character. His reputation had even ridden farther than Jim Silver himself had gone.

As he came in sight of the Chester ranch house—a long, low building of unpainted boards—he put the sombrero back on his head, and he was glad of a little pool of dust that whirled down on the wind and tarnished the brilliance of Parade with gray.

When he got up to the ranch house, he tethered the horse, went to the kitchen door, and rapped.

The door was jerked open, and a woman with a red, weary face, hot from cookery, appeared before him.

She exclaimed: "Another one of you lazy, worthless rascals that calls yourselves cowboys! I'd fire every last one of you off the' place, if I had my way about it. It's a crying pity, I tell Will Chester, to waste good money on the feeding of them that are no better than tramps!"

Silver had tipped his hat, and now he settled it slowly back on his head.

He would have been glad to do away with the embarrassing notoriety of his celebrated name, but he hardly liked being called a tramp.

"Mrs. Chester," he said, "I'm not a tramp."

She thrust out her big red fist.

"Lemme see your hand, young man!" she demanded.

He surrendered his hand, and she rubbed a thumb over the palm of it.

"Just as I thought!" she shouted. "Soft as the hand of a girl! And yet you call yourself a cow-puncher, do you?

55

You got the nerve to stand there and call yourself a working man, an honest man?"

"Well," said Silver gently, "a fellow can be honest, even if he doesn't punch cows, can't he?"

"Honest doing what?" exclaimed Mrs. Chester. "Honest, my foot! Honest men have calluses on their hands, or else they're living on stolen money, is what I say. But fetch your lazy hulk in here and set down at the table, while I get you some food. A pity, I say, though, when a woman can't be the boss in her own kitchen, but has to foller the crazy ways of her husband. Spendthrift is what he is. Spendthrift!"

"I only want to see a man who's working here," said he. "I'd like to see Alec Gary, if you know where he can be found."

"How would I know where he could be found?" she demanded. "Hurry up and come inside before all the flies in the world get into the kitchen. Ain't you got no sense at all?"

He stepped inside, removing his hat.

"There—set down at that table," she commanded. "I'll fetch you some cold pone and some cold boiled beef, to fill yourself with. There's no coffee, this time of day, but tea is—"

"Thanks," said Silver. "I don't need anything to eat. I only want to find Alec Gary, if you'll tell me where he's probably working on the ranch."

"Alec? How would you come to know a good, hardworking, honest boy like Alec?" she asked suspiciously. "What you want with him?"

"His uncle has died," said Silver.

"A good riddance," answered Mrs. Chester. "The great, hulking, cruel brute. There ain't going to be no tears shed about his death. Not in no part of the world there ain't!"

She had stepped back toward the stove, as she said this, and glancing out the kitchen window, she saw the great stallion at the hitch rack. The wind was blowing through his mane and tail, and his head was high, to look into the breeze at that moment. What Mrs. Chester saw made her turn and stare again at Silver, and he felt her eyes fix above his upon the telltale patches of gray on his temples, the hornlike spots of silver that had given him his nickname all through the world.

"Good heavens!" said Mrs. Chester. She picked up the skirt of her apron and folded her red hands inside it. "Good heavens, what have I been saying? Are you Jim Silver?"

He silently cursed the folly that had induced him to enter the kitchen where he had to take off his hat. But now he had to admit: "Yes, that's my name. Alec Gary is—"

"He's down the creek, mending fence," said she. "Mr. Silver, what'll you be thinking about a fool of a woman that—"

"Hush!" said Jim Silver, smiling. "You were perfectly right. I don't know how many years have gone by since I've done an honest stroke of work."

He got out to Parade, escaping from the apologies of Mrs. Chester as well as he could, and she remained staring after him, screening her eyes from the sun with one hand until he was well down the line of the creek.

A mile from the ranch house he found a tall cowpuncher toiling over a big-handled borer with which he was drilling a series of post holes. His hat was off. His curling black hair shuddered in the sunlight with the violence of his efforts. It was the perfect picture of a man doing disagreeable work with all his might, and striving as hard for wages as though for his own interests.

He looked up as Silver drew near, and Jim Silver was relieved to see a fine, open face and an excellently shaped head. He had feared that he would look on a type like that dead savage of the mountains, Bill Gary.

He dismounted, saying: "You're Alec Gary? My name is Silver. I've brought you bad news and good news together. The bad part is that your uncle, Bill Gary, is dead."

He waited curiously to see the reaction, and saw the brow of Alec Gary pucker.

"Are you Jim Silver?" asked Gary. "Then," he added, as Silver nodded, "I suppose this is one of the first times in your life that you've ever brought a man bad news. It *is* bad news to me. Uncle Bill was a hard man, but he was pretty good to me."

Silver nodded. "I'm glad to hear that," he said. "I'll follow up with the good news, if good is what you call it. This is a copy of a letter that he wrote as he was dying. The copy runs to the point where he must have stopped writing because he died. It was a wolf that killed him. He was badly torn, Gary."

Young Alec Gary took the paper which Silver held out and scanned it carefully. He stared up into Silver's face with amazement.

"A gold mine!" he exclaimed. And for one instant the yellow flame of the gold hunger burned wildly in his eyes. Then he groaned. "Inside the collar, and on the neck of Frosty! It might as well be tied to the neck of a thunderbolt, as far as I'm concerned."

"Suppose," said Silver, "that we both try our hands on him."

"You?" said Gary. "Would you help? Why, Mr. Silver, if you will help me, of course we'll make an even split on the profits."

"I get profits of my own," said Silver, "and I can't take a share of anything that comes out of this."

"Why not?" asked Alec Gary, amazed.

"Because I've made a resolution, long ago, never to handle blood money."

"Blood money? This isn't a price on a man's head."

"No," said Silver. "It's a price that your uncle has already paid. If the mine goes to you, it's all right. If I share in it, the ghost of Bill Gary will haunt me. Let's find Chester and ask him if you can cut loose for a few weeks. Or maybe it will be months. There is a great deal that we have to talk over—and the first thing is Frosty."

CHAPTER X

The Hunter

CHRISTIAN went to Joe Thurston. It was on record that Joe Thurston had killed a running deer at eight hundred yards. There was no doubt about the fact, and though a good many of the old-time hunters were likely to say that nothing but luck could account for such marksmanship, there were others who said that a man like Thurston never had luck. He was simply one of the few past masters.

But Thurston spent most of his time not in hunting with a rifle, but with a pack of dogs. To support that pack and to follow it afield, he had allowed his big ranch to go to pieces. The one thing that he valued in life, outside of an occasional brawl in a saloon, was a chance to see his pack corner a wild beast and tear it to pieces, or at least hold it at bay until his rifle settled the argument.

Joe Thurston was himself a wild beast, and perhaps that was why he understood the ways of the wilderness so very well. He was a little man, very dark, very handsome when he smiled, and very sinister when, in silence, he allowed his upper lip to curl a little.

He sat, on this day, on the back of a young brown

gelding which he had just finished breaking. Blood was still trickling down the gored sides of the horse, and blood-stained, also, the froth that dripped from the wounded mouth of the gelding, for Thurston used a cruel spade bit that opened up like a sword when the rider jerked on the reins. A horse, for Thurston, was simply a machine that got him from one place to another. He despised sentimentality. It was not in his nature. He was forty-five. He looked a full ten or even fifteen years younger. But as many years as he had gained, his poor wife had lost. He looked more like her son than her husband.

He was overlooking the feeding of his pack. They were fed once a day, in the middle of the afternoon, and they got little, from one end of the year to the other, except raw meat. If one of them fell sick, it rarely received medicine. Either nature cured it, or soon it was brained and its carcass fed to the ravenous pack.

That pack was always ravenous. Joe Thurston knew exactly how the dogs should be fed in order to keep them in the pink of condition, thin until they were as keen as edged swords for game and food, but not thin enough to be weakened.

Barry Christian and Gregor came up at that moment and waved to the keeper of the pack.

"Are you Joe Thurston?" Christian said.

Thurston failed to turn his head. His mood was savage that afternoon. Ordinarily, he would have given some heed to a pair of big, powerful, well-mounted fellows like Christian and Gregor, but on this day he had in mind the pressing demands of certain creditors. Already his ranch was heavily mortgaged, and now it seemed that it would be wiped out. He cared nothing about the loss of land and cattle, but with the other possessions his pack would go, also. And that was a knife in his heart.

"I'm Joe Thurston," he admitted shortly.

"My name is Barry Christian," said the outlaw.

"The devil it is," answered Thurston.

"And this is Duff Gregor," said Christian.

The head of Thurston slowly turned. He looked over the pale, clean lines of the face of Christian and at the bright, thoughtful eyes. They were a little too bright, in fact. Suddenly Thurston knew that it was Christian, indeed. And he could not help smiling. There was so much evil, so much violence in his own nature that he suddenly felt something expand and lighten in his heart.

He held out his hand, silently, and took the strong grip of the criminal. He shook hands with Duff Gregor, also, and saw that the man was a nonentity compared with his more celebrated companion. And yet any one who had dared, more than once, to play the rôle of Jim Silver, was worthy of some attention.

"Want something here?" asked Thurston.

"Yes," said Christian, "I want you and your dogs."

"Ah?" said Thurston.

"I'm going to hunt wolves," said Christian.

The door of the house slammed. Christian saw a girl with a face pale as stone, and shadowy, great eyes, come out on the back porch and look toward him. She turned, and reëntered the house again.

"Inviting me or hiring me?" asked Thurston.

"Inviting you," said Christian.

Thurston took a quick breath. Rage had been mounting in his throat, tightening like a fist inside his gullet. Now the passion left him.

"I've hunted wolves before," said he noncommittally. "Where do you want to pick them up?"

"In the Blue Waters, or the foothills near them," said Christian.

"That's a hard country," said Thurston. "Are you talking about Frosty?"

"That's the only wolf I've ever wanted to catch," said Christian.

Thurston narrowed his eyes.

"There's a price on the head of that wolf," he remarked.

"I'm not hunting for the price. That goes to you. Besides, I'll add something over and above. A thousand dollars, say."

"Well?" murmured Thurston, pinching his lips together in a smile. "I understand that Jim Silver is down there in the Blue Waters—doing good for humanity again—hunting for Frosty, the cattle thief."

"Silver is there," agreed the outlaw. "That's why I want to be there. To meet him on his own ground."

"Haven't there been times," said grim Joe Thurston, "when you weren't so glad to meet Jim Silver on any ground?"

"He's had the upper hand more than once," answered Christian. "But the fact is that there isn't room on top of the earth for the two of us. One of us has to be buried, and the time has come.

"He's in the Blue Waters hunting a wolf. Well, I'm going to be there hunting a wolf. He has a man with him. I have Gregor. If we happen to meet along the trail, it's no business of yours. Gregor and I will have to try to tend to that part of the game."

"I don't follow this," said Thurston. "Unless you mean that it's a challenge to Jim Silver—something to make him come hunting for *you?*"

"You can call it that. If he comes for me, he has to meet me on my own ground. And I won't be asleep."

"It looks to me," said Thurston, "as though there might be something in this deal. I'll go one step farther. I'll admit that I need the money. That thousand—"

"I'll pay half of it on the nail the moment we shake hands," said Christian, "and the other half the instant that Frosty's dead at my feet."

"What'll you do with him?" asked Thurston curiously.

"Mount the hide. Send it somewhere to stand behind glass. A proof to people that I've beaten Silver at at least one job."

Thurston actually laughed aloud.

"Here's my hand on the deal," he exclaimed.

Christian shook the hand. He pulled out a wallet and counted five hundred-dollar bills and put them in the fingers of Thurston.

"That binds the deal," he said.

"I'll write up the contract," said Thurston.

"We've shaken hands," said Christian, "and that's enough."

A dull flush of pleasure worked in the face of Thurston.

"Besides," exclaimed Christian, in his gentle and persuasive voice, the very accent of courtesy, "you can't draw up a contract between yourself and Barry Christian. You can't make a contract with an outlawed man. To you, my name is simply Wilkins, and this is Murphy." He broke off to add: "I'd like to see the pack."

"Use your eyes," said Thurston, whose own politeness could not last long. He waved toward the big pens that contained the dogs.

"I don't know enough about them to see the whole truth," answered Christian.

Thurston glanced at him with an appreciative flash of the eye.

"Few men with brains enough to say they don't know," said Thurston. "Come along with me."

He moved down the line of the pens.

"There's the brains of the pack," he said, pointing to a number of big, rangy pointers. "People use 'em to find birds. I use 'em to find coyotes and wolves and mountain lions. They've got the best noses in the world. They're fast, and they can run all day. I've bred 'em for speed and nose and brain. Those pointers would never point a bird in a thousand years, but they'll point a wolf. What's more, they'll hold the trail on a wolf. Yes, or a mountain lion. Whatever they've been entered on."

"What's wrong with them?" asked Christian.

"Why do you ask?"

"Nothing is perfect."

Thurston grinned.

"They're too hot-headed and tender. They want to rush in and get their teeth into the game, and the wolves or the big cats open 'em up like fried beefsteak."

He went to another set of pens where were housed some of the biggest greyhounds that Christian had ever seen. They moved around with little, stilted steps, as though their muscles were sore. They were tucked up into bows. Their chests were narrow. The shoulders and thighs were overlaid with entangled whipcords.

"They're the point of the arrow," he said. "They'll run

63

down any wolf that ever breathed almost two steps for one. If the pointers get a wolf into open sight, this gang will get up in time to mob him and hold him back until the heavy artillery gets into action. And here's the heavy artillery."

He indicated the next pens, where there were dogs built and furred like Scottish deerhounds, but enormously bigger. They looked made for speed and strength of running, but also there was a terrible promise in the size of the muzzles, the fangs, the huge muscles along the jaws.

"Every one of 'em," said Christian with keen interest, "looks able to do for a wolf."

"Some of 'em could kill a buffalo wolf now and then," agreed Thurston, watching the monsters with a hungry eye. "But some wolves are mean devils in a fight. No matter what's the breed or the training of a dog, a wolf seems to have more biting powers and more fighting brains and tricks. However, I'll match two of these dogs against the biggest wolf that ever lived, and three of 'em will kill the champion of the wolf world—even if his name is Frosty!"

He nodded with assurance as he said this, adding, "This breed was started by Bill Gary. You may happen to know him since you know Frosty. Frosty was what killed Gary, people say. I don't know how the story started. But Gary never managed to get out of his own stock what I've done with it. He didn't use enough persistence, enough time and money on the job. I don't care where the wolf is, I'll catch him with this pack. In open country or foothills it will be a joke. In the middle of the mountains I'll catch him or run him to earth. Frosty's hide is as good as mounted and behind glass, Christian, this very minute!"

CHAPTER XI

Frosty's Mate

SHE was tall. She was beautiful. She moved with a light and delicate grace. There was bright humor and good nature in her eyes. She was young. She was gay. She was foolish. And Frosty loved her the moment he set eyes on her in the moonlight of that glade.

Wolf song had been in the air for a long time that night, and there were notes in the singing that made Frosty wrinkle his nose and point his head at the sky and break that inviolable rule of silence which had been his for a year— since the days of his puppyhood, in fact. Now he opened his throat, and his immense bass note went booming through the canyons among the softer singing of the wind and the rumble and hollow crashing of cataracts which had been newly loosened from the long, white silence of the winter. Spring was in the air.

Frosty had not seen enough springs to know what it was that worked like electric fire through his blood. But it was a thing that called him in hot haste to that mountain gorge where five big wolves moved slowly around this cream of wolf beauty, this sleek, well-furred lady of the hills.

Frosty came swiftly. He fell in love while he was still on the run, literally, and so he continued his charge. He did not even pause to touch noses with the lady and inquire after her health and happiness. He simply ran berserk among those wolves.

In fact, Frosty had been laid up all this time in order to be healed of the wounds that he had received while he was in the jaws of the trap. He was now completely recovered, and the thick fur had closed well over the scars. But he was hungry. He had been living on rabbits he had managed to surprise, on unwary squirrels, on mice above all. He was hungry, too, for a dash of excitement. And five wolves looked just about the right number to give him a good fight, he felt.

He gave one such a tremendous shoulder wallop that the big lobo rolled a dozen yards away and let out the yell of fear and of defeat. He dived straight on under the throat of another and slashed him deeply across the breast. He nearly ripped the hamstring out of the next, and laid open the head of the fourth hero from eye to muzzle. The fifth timber wolf had seen enough, and took to his heels. The others followed as fast as they could, while Frosty, laughing his wide, red laughter, lay down and licked the blood from his white vest, and from his forelegs and forepaws. He was a very dainty and clean-living fellow, was Frosty.

The pleasure of that brief skirmish had not yet rollicked out of his heart when he saw that the lady of his dreams was sitting on a hummock with her beautiful long, bushy tail curled around her forepaws. The moment he glanced at her she rose, turned, and fled.

He followed.

She was as fast as a deer, and she went down the wind as though the devil of wolves were after her. But, fast as she was, he was a little bit faster.

Suddenly she whirled, her mane bristling, her ears twitched back, her eyes green with hatred, her fangs bared.

Frosty walked right up to that dreadful mask of hatred and sniffed at her nose. And then, suddenly, they stood back from one another and laughed two red laughters, set off with teeth that glistened just like ice.

66

There are no tears at the wedding ceremony of a wolf. They seem to have a saving sense of humor, and so there was only a great deal of that silent laughter at the marriage of Frosty under the spring moon.

Kind Mother Nature had brought to him a proper mate, and he could have looked his life long among the ladies of his kind before he would have found one more handsome, more discreet, more prepared to learn the wisdom of hunting laws and ways.

She had been well raised, as wolf rearing goes. She was not the least bit of a fool, and she knew as well as a Greek philosopher that the track of grizzly is not one to follow, and that foxes are too swift to be caught, and that their wits are even sharper than their teeth. She knew that mountain sheep are better avoided than troubled, and that small pickings will eventually make a full belly.

She knew the rain signs and the wind signs that the god of wolves hangs in the midnight blue of the sky, and she could read like type the scents that travel on the breeze. But in all the bright days of her life she never had tasted either beef or horse, and sheep were unknown to her except when the well-guarded flocks went by at a distance, always accompanied by the distressing scent of man, the great enemy, and gunpowder and steel.

When Frosty discovered that she was afraid of going out of the highlands into the hills, he sat down and looked her in the face. Then he stood up and jogged quietly on his way along the down trail.

She turned and went the other way, until she found out that he would no longer follow. Then she whined like a dog for him, and afterward she sang a mournful tune. Last of all, she got to her feet and raced like the wind to catch up with him, picking his scent off the ground and then out of the air until she was at his side once more.

He merely turned his head a little and admitted that he was aware of her coming. For he had a very good domestic and political head, did Frosty, and he knew as well as any wolf in the world how to be the head of a family.

So they came out into the foothills, and Frosty headed straight for the biggest, the choicest, of all of his preserves.

It was a ranch where there were cattle *and* sheep; where there were plenty of pigs and chickens, and a creamery, and poultry, including ducks and turkeys and geese, and there were rabbits, white and brown, and there were goats and beef cattle big and small, and horses, and mules, and nearly every sort of four-footed beast that one could imagine on a big Western ranch.

It was the Truman place, with an almost national reputation behind it. But Frosty, in a sense, knew that place better than even its wise-headed owner. He had tasted of every sort of meat that his unwilling host could provide, and his track was so well-known that drawings and photographs and measurements of the tracks of Frosty were to be found in the study of John Truman. That was not all. Mrs. Truman was a very clever artist with her pencil, and several times she had seen the terrible Frosty—by starlight, by moonlight, in the dusk, and in the crystal pink of the early morning light. So she had done a number of pictures of the monster, and, in fact, Frosty was a major item of conversation in the Truman household.

It was not accident that when Frosty came out of the mountains to dine in high estate, his mate beside him, he should have traveled straight toward the greatest of danger. It was not accident, because something far from chance had brought Barry Christian and Duff Gregor and the famous pack of the Thurston dogs to the ranch of Truman.

It was known that Truman would do almost anything in the world to get rid of the cunning marauder. There was some risk that he might recognize Christian, but, as a matter of fact, he proved to be blind to everything except the manifest excellence of the dog pack of Joe Thurston. He was glad to house that pack and feed it gratis, and he hoped that Thurston would continue to stay at his house, even for a year and a day, and enjoy free board for his pack, so long as the chief business of that pack continued to be the hunting of Frosty.

They sat in the house, the four of them, and looked at the photographs of the sign of Frosty, and admired the clever drawings which Mrs. Truman had made of the devastator himself. And while they were laying their plans and deciding in what direction they had better cast through the hills and into the mountains in the hope of finding the trail of the great wolf, Frosty in person was sliding through the fence of the southeastern section and heading straight toward the house, followed by his frightened mate.

She was, in fact, fairly blind with fear.

But she was also hungry, and when she came to a fresh-killed carcass she said:

"That meat is new and good. And I have an empty stomach."

Frosty shuddered till his mane stood up on end.

Dead meat? Eat dead meat? Not since he was a puppy —not since he had become a wolf of the world and had learned how to set his own table properly.

But he decided to give her a lesson. So he took her right up into the wind toward the new kill, and then lay down and bade her study the scents.

A pair of coyotes, frightened from the feast, fled far away. But Frosty paid no heed to them.

"Death is not a nothing," he said. "There is always a reason. Sometimes it is the odor of gunpowder and the steel of man. Sometimes the teeth of other hunters have done the work. And sometimes it is the work of poison such as I have seen kill big wolves, and wise and strong wolves. A small tooth will kill the biggest wolf in the world if it strikes him in the right place. Poison is such a strong tooth as that. It cannot be seen. But it can be tasted, and, above all, it can be smelled.

"Now hold your head straight up and sniff the air— smell the fresh blood from where the coyotes have been feeding. And in that you find an acrid taint. That is poison. It will kill those coyotes. It will surely kill them. I have seen a mountain lion in such an agony that it leaped at the grizzly of Thunder Mountain in the middle of its fit from the poison. And the grizzly, of course, smashed the head of that big cat with one stroke of his paw.

"Now, to prove that I know of what I speak, come with me and you shall see a thing."

He took her around the carcass of the dead calf and

across the big field to the edge of a dry draw. Rapid, light feet scampered away from a place where the stars fell bright and small in a little water hole.

"After poison, hunters drink," said Frosty. "Now watch!"

The two coyotes had climbed to the farther side of the draw when one of them stopped, whirled suddenly, and snapped at the empty air. The wolves could hear the teeth clash like steel against steel. The other coyote drew back and sat down to watch.

"Poison!" said Frosty. "And now he is fighting an enemy that he cannot see. Look!"

The coyote had leaped up into the air, and, falling again, it twisted into a frightful convulsion. Its mate, a moment later, was caught by the same fits. In the fury of their silent agonies, it seemed as though they were fighting one another in the midst of the thin cloud of dust that they raised.

Then the two were still. One lay perfectly still on its side. The other was braced up on its forelegs, but the hindquarters trailed on the ground as though paralyzed.

And as a small breeze moved the air, the two wolves found in it again the strange, the indescribable scent of the invisible death. Frosty's mate shrank suddenly against his side, and she snarled:

"Let us go! Quickly! Quickly! Every wise wolf knows that men are dangerous, and that they can bite from far away. Let us go. I had rather have a few field mice in peace of mind than all the beef banquets of this world of men."

CHAPTER XII

The Kill

It was very good reasoning that the lady had applied to that question, but Frosty only laughed his red laughter. He looked at the beauty of his mate and remembered her speed of foot and all the cleverness that she had showed along the trail, and he felt a great happiness, because he knew that he was going to have a proper audience to appreciate his efforts.

He said to her: "Men have their own keen ways. So have mice and squirrels, for that matter. And so has Frosty. Come with me!"

The scent of the poison and the sight of what it could accomplish had made her almost sick with fear, but she followed Frosty slowly across the fields, and then he showed her some good hunting.

The wind came always in puffs, slowly and gently, the very best sort of a wind for the carrying of scents of every kind, and, getting to the right quarter of the compass, Frosty worked up that wind to the edge of a big field where a great mound of something living slept upon the ground.

"Beef?" said his mate.

"Ours!" said Frosty, and since the wires of that fence were strung close together and wickedly barbed, he leaped lightly and trotted on.

Over his shoulder he saw her slenderer body follow, arching against the stars, and he was immensely pleased to see this blind faith in her. But he paused to give her a caution.

"This is a trick," said Frosty, "which I have learned. But it has cost a good many other wolves their lives. It is all a matter of foot and eye and tooth and quick thinking. I have seen three wolves gored to death in this game—yes, and each time they were hunting in packs. Perhaps they were a little too hungry to have clear wits. Sit down and watch me work. That is a bull yonder, and a bull fights to the last gasp. One thing is to make the kill swiftly, because a bull roars as he fights. And then men come on horses!"

"Ugh!" shuddered his mate. "The wind changes, and I smell dogs and the scent of many men."

"There are always dogs about this place," said Frosty carelessly. "The trouble with dogs is that when they can run fast enough to catch you, they have no jaw muscles for biting. And when they are big enough to take a grip, they are too clumsy to put a tooth on a wolf that has his wits about him. Besides, the fools are easily made to change their minds."

He thought, as he said that, of the two great dogs of the trapper that had *not* been made to change their minds till they were dead. And back in his mind there was the memory of a certain great mastiff that, in the midst of a mob scene, had once managed to lay its deadly grip on Frosty. The pain of the wound ached right up into the back of his mind as he recalled it.

His mate obediently sat down. He could see the stars in her bright eyes, and it made him laugh to observe her fear. However, she said nothing. Only the fur of her mane lifted as she saw him actually turn toward that monstrous antagonist.

He went up softly toward that mountain of dangerous

72

flesh. There had been a night when he had slit the throat of a sleeping steer just as it tossed up its head. Perhaps he would have equal luck on this occasion and make the battle end in blessed silence. However, he was not surprised when the big brute lurched suddenly from the ground, rear end first, and swung to face him. For a range bull is only a shade less wary than any meat eater, and fully as savage.

This was the hardy veteran of a score of battles with his kind, a true champion of the range. He got the wind of Frosty, came to his feet like a wild cat, and charged without even waiting to bellow.

He missed Frosty.

The she-wolf did not rise from her haunches. She remained in the near distance, lolling her tongue, apparently indifferent. In reality, she was taking stock of her mate's talent as a provider. She saw Frosty avoid that thrusting of sharp horns, swing to the side, and sway back again to get behind the monster.

But the bull was wary, and spun about in time.

He put down his head and pawed the earth, preparing to bellow. Frosty made a bluff of charging straight at the head and lowered horns. It was a very good bluff. It looked to the watcher as though her mate were hurling himself right on those terrible, curved spear points. The bull took three little running steps to meet the shock—and Frosty floated away to the side, slid like a ghost under the belly of the bull, and danced away on the farther side.

The bull whirled again. Muttering thunder was forming in his throat. The she-wolf heard it, and she smelled fresh blood—beef blood. She could even hear it trickling to the ground, splashing in a pool. Frosty had used his teeth in that last maneuver.

He was ready to use them again. He went in at that huge bull like a snipe flying against the wind. The bull backed, checked, charged furiously. In the dullness of the starlight high overhead, the she-wolf saw the clots of turf flying. The ground trembled with the beating of the hoofs.

The horns missed Frosty by a margin so slight that the bull paused to hook two or three times at the spot in the air where the gray wolf had seemed to be. Then he jerked up his head with an almost human groan of pain, for Frosty, twisting about to the rear, had chopped right through the great tendon over the hock as cleanly as a butcher could have done with a sharp cleaver.

The bull started to spin, but it was hard to maneuver rapidly on only one rear leg, and the she-wolf heard the dull, chopping sound as the great fangs of Frosty struck through the tendon of the other leg.

The bull dropped to his hind quarters, still formidable, for with the sway of his monstrous horns he could guard his flanks; in the meantime, out of his throat rolled a thundering call of rage, and appeal, and helplessness.

Frosty sat down five yards away to laugh, as though he enjoyed that music, but in the middle of the lowing he flashed off his feet and dipped right in under the stretched-out throat of the bull. He cut that throat wide open across the tender narrows just beneath the jaws. The bull, trying to bellow again, only belched forth a vast stream of blood.

Frosty went back and stood beside his mate, panting:

"That was easy. You see how it's done. Just a little matter of foot and eye and tooth."

She put her shoulder against him and shuddered. And the heart of Frosty grew great. He suddenly felt as though he would rejoice in a chance to bring red meat home to a wife and cubs. Yes, to dozens of them!

The bull, slumping suddenly forward, struck the earth in a loose, dead bulk. Now he was still, and the banquet table was spread!

The she-wolf delayed only to see her mate put tooth to the hide. Then she was instantly at work.

Frosty was hungry; he was very hungry. It was a long time since he had had a chance to enjoy the sort of diet that he relished most, but all of his hunger and all this delicious smell of fresh blood could not hide in his mind the knowledge that he was dining on the very verge of destruction. So, while his wife tore out great gobbets and whole pounds of tender flesh, Frosty ate more daintily, more delicately.

Now and again he would lift his great, wise young head and survey the country around him, and the obscure line

74

where the starlit sky met the thicker night of the earth. It took eyes and some knowing to observe the movement of forms at a distance against such a background. But, when danger threatened a moment later, it took nothing but ears and nose to understand.

It was the scent of man and dogs in the distance, and the sound of a man calling, and the answering high *yip-yipping* of the dogs.

Inside the house of Truman they had been talking late, smoking, telling old tales of hunting, listening to Thurston's description of some of the great runs the pack had made; and then, out of the distance, they heard the booming, thundering call of the bull.

Truman got out of this chair at once, crossed the room, and opened a window wide. He leaned into the night and listened. The bellowing of the bull was cut off short. In the middle of the great, angry lament the thunder ended.

Truman turned back to the others.

"There's something wrong," he said. "That's a mighty expensive bull I've got out yonder, and I don't like the way he cut off that bellow, as though somebody had just laid a whip on him!"

Christian said: "Maybe it's Frosty come down to dine."

Truman shook his head. "It won't be Frosty," he said. "Frosty wouldn't waste as much effort as that killing old beef when there's so much young stuff scattered around the place. He'd rather have veal than beef. I know his tastes."

He leaned out through the window again, shaking his head, very worried.

Thurston stood up and said:

"I'll take a walk with a few of my dogs and see what I can turn up."

"No good doing that," answered Truman. "No good trying to run that devil of a wolf in the dark of the moon, and he very well knows it."

Thurston turned and smiled. It was not a real smile, but merely a baring of the teeth.

"You're rather proud of what your Blue Waters wolf can do, Truman," he said, "but I'll tell you this: My pack

75

will find in the dark and it will run in the dark, and it will kill in the dark, too. If friend Frosty is anywhere around, he's a dead wolf before morning."

With that Joe Thurston walked out of the house and got his selection from the dogs. He simply took a pair of pointers so perfectly trained that they would obey gestures as far as the wave of the hand could be seen. Whistles could give them further orders.

Barry Christian walked out with Thurston and the dogs into the field, and saw, almost at once, the outline of the bulk of the bull, prostrate. Asleep, perhaps, as Barry Christian thought. But then the dogs, scouting close to the bull, failed to rouse it to its feet, which was strange, and a moment later the pointers were kiting across the field and giving trouble.

"Wolves, by thunder!" shouted Thurston.

His whistle shrilled into the night to call back the pointers before they ran themselves into hopeless trouble.

"Come back to the house!" he shouted to Christian. "We'll saddle up and hit the trail."

Christian had lighted a match close to the bull. He saw the terribly torn throat; he saw a big patch of blood, and in the softness of the ground that was outlined, the huge print of a wolf's foot, a print so big that it started his heart racing.

"Thurston!" he cried. "We've got on his trail at last. It's Frosty, or his twin!"

CHAPTER XIII

The Chase

WHEN Frosty heard the outbreak of the dogs and the voice of the man, he had to snap his big teeth close to the head of his mate before she would leave off her greedy feeding and lift her red, dripping muzzle.

"A full stomach makes a slow foot," he told her. "Come! Let us go!"

She was reluctant. He urged her with the powerful thrust of his shoulder, and at last she slunk away, regretfully, slackening her pace every now and then. He studied her with a critical eye. She had eaten like fire. Already she was logey with food. She ran with her head down, and her tail down, also. She kept coughing, and she stumbled over small obstacles.

Behind them the noise of the dogs and the man ceased. Then it came once more, and a pair of dogs rushed straight at Frosty through the starlight. He turned back to get ready for them, merely saying to his mate:

"Guard my heels and I'll take them. Guard my back and I'll handle them."

No matter how unfit she might be for battle, she fell in

behind him and faced to guard his back. But the two big dogs that came glimmering out of the starlight veered off to this side and that. They retreated to a little distance and howled.

Both Frosty and his mate charged the pair. The pointers turned and fled faster than the wolves could follow. For a timber wolf is not very fleet of foot. He is made for endurance and the shock of hard fighting, not for flight, like the fox or the coyote. Only in the rough country of the uplands will a timber wolf pull away from a pack of dogs. The she-wolf managed to slash the hip of one of the dogs; that was all.

Then she turned with Frosty and started to race off at full speed. He calmed her and made her come back to a dogtrot. For it was plain that she could not stand the test of a hard run at once. Frosty himself was not exactly comfortable, for there was a considerable burden of meat inside him, and yet he had eaten nothing in comparison with his companion. Her sides thrust out with her meal. Her panting was a painful thing to hear.

It was better to go on rather slowly, always in the direction of the higher foothills and the mountains beyond them.

"We are safe, anyway," said the she-wolf. "We are safe, because there are only two dogs, and they can do us no harm. I laughed to see how they ran."

"There is the scent of man in the air, and you know that always means danger."

"It is from the collar that you wear, like a dog, around your neck," said his mate, sniffing at the linked steel.

He tossed his head, and the collar slid a little upward through his fur. Already he had some cause to be grateful for the protection it had given to him, for in the battle that won him his mate, the second big wolf had struck for the throat of Frosty, and merely snapped a fang short off on the metal that ran around his throat. For all that, it was a hateful thing, because it continually reminded him of the most dreadful moment of his life.

Still, he could not conceive what had happened after the blow that had knocked him senseless. During the interval, in the darkness of his mind, the steel teeth of the trap

78

had been removed from his hind leg and the steel bondage of the collar had been placed around his neck. The man had withdrawn and sat against a tree, bleeding. And he, Frosty, had been free to escape.

Sometimes he felt as though that collar were man's claim upon him, a detached hand that had him by the throat, and by which he might be one day throttled, as he had seen a brute of a wolf trapper once throttle a litter of helpless young puppies at the mouth of a cave. Or perhaps a mysterious agency was attracted to the steel and would one day draw him back to mysterious man.

They got out of the low, rolling ground and climbed to the top of the first steep rise, where the she-wolf flung herself down on the ground suddenly. She was sick, and she could hardly travel farther.

"Only," she gasped, "only a fool runs from a memory. Only a fool runs from a shadow."

Frosty looked down at her heaving sides. Then he scanned the dark shadow of the lower ground beneath him. It might be, in fact, that no more danger was coming toward them, though in that case it was very strange that the two dogs, alone, dared to remain so close. Here they were again, glimmering shapes in the starlight, and pausing at a little distance, they sat down to howl at the enemy. The lips of Frosty twitched as he considered the keen edge of his teeth and the softness of their throats, but he was not a witless one to try to catch four faster feet than his own.

Then out of the distance he heard a deadly chorus. There were more voices like those of the pointers. He could hear the keen yelping of the greyhounds, thin and far away, and, above all, the harsh cries of dogs whose voices were exactly like those of the ugly pair of monsters that had fallen upon him when he was in the trap.

There were more than a score of throats giving music to that chorus. The heart of Frosty suddenly grew small in him. He stood over his mate and said to her:

"Do you hear?"

"It is far away," she panted huskily.

"It is pointing toward us, and the yelling of these two

79

dogs holds the light on us like a shaft of sunshine, and guides the others. They are coming rapidly. Up, up! Away with me!"

She rose with a lurch so slow and so heavy that the heart of Frosty failed in him again. Certainly she was hard spent, and yet the worst of the run might remain all ahead of them. In this condition he dared not lead her at a rapid pace. He could merely pick rough going, always, so that their trail would furnish as much difficulty as possible to the dogs in the distance.

But what great difference did the trailing make when the two pointers, always near by, guided their companions out of the night with their outcry?

Moreover, the gray of the morning began now, streaking around the rim of the horizon and making the mountains stand up black and huge against the eastern sky.

With terrible speed the clamor from the rear rolled up on them. He saw his mate swing her head in impatient fear from side to side, hunting some escape.

"We must hide! We must hide!" she gasped.

"They have noses that will find us," said Frosty.

"Then we can fight them away from some narrow place," said the she-wolf.

"Man kills from afar," said Frosty.

"Run far ahead then," she said. "Let me stay here behind. I am sick. My knees are weak, and my hocks will not bear me up. Run ahead, and I shall handle myself."

He fell in behind her and nipped at her heels.

"Little fool!" said Frosty, and drove her relentlessly before him up the way.

The wind brought to them the smell of a barnyard, of man, and the thin, distant clamor of more dogs. The she-wolf would have swerved to the side, but Frosty drove her straight ahead.

Of ordinary dogs he had no heed whatever. But those keen yelpings of the greyhounds from the rear he understood. Even the antelope could hardly run faster than those lean beasts. He had seen them overtake and kill the wing-footed rabbits. And once they came in sight of their target, nothing could keep them from overtaking a pair of wolves, particularly wolves running in the open.

Worst of all, there was the harsh calling of greater throats, giving forth notes like those of the two monsters which had come before Bill Gary to the traps.

Frosty felt cornered, though still at a distance. The steel hand of man was surely closing about his throat. And it seemed to Frosty that the collar was shrinking, shutting off his breath.

He paid no heed, therefore, to the smell of the barnyard and the scent of man and the yelping of other dogs. He even welcomed the thing and drove his unwilling mate before him straight down into a hollow where stood the long, squat shadow of a ranch house and the larger mass of a barn behind it.

"There will be confusion down there," he told her. "Geese will cackle, and hens and ducks. Dogs will howl. The scents of a hundred cattle will cross our trail. Perhaps we shall be able to sneak away to safety across the dangerous ground."

But he had no very great hope of that. He only knew that he would be safe if he took to his heels and left his mate behind him to be torn by the teeth of the pack.

He could not do that. The power of instinct checked and held him powerfully to her. He was not one to change his mind when danger threatened.

So they came down into the hollow, and as they reached the damper, colder air below, they heard the forefront of the dog pack break over the hill behind them—the pointers first, and then the greyhounds on the leash, and then the fighting heavy artillery of the crew. Worst of all, there were beating hoofs of horses, and the calling of men to one another. And always the cursed daylight brightened around the rim of the wide horizon.

He saw the entangled mazes of corral fencing behind him. He turned, and, with a determined charge, drove the two pointers who were closest far away from him. They yielded ground readily, as always. While they lingered in the distance, he whirled about and leaped the nearest fence. His mate had already crawled under the lowest wire, and was disappearing around the corner of a great stack of hay that stood in the middle of the inclosure.

A little yellow dog came scooting toward him, yapping at the top of its lungs, splitting the night with its sharp *ki-yiing*. He swerved toward it. The house dog, terrified by the size and the imminence of that danger, dropped flat on the ground.

One stroke of his teeth and Frosty would leave it with a smashed back, dead. But he disdained an enemy of such proportions, and hurried on as fast as he could leg it, until, turning the corner of the haystack, he was amazed to find that there was no sight of his mate before him!

No, not although his glance could now extend far across the fields brightened with dew.

He dropped his bewildered head toward the ground and suddenly picked up her trail. It turned sharply to the side into one of the hollows that were worked under the side of the haystack, where cattle had fed and where scratching chickens had widened the entrances. Into one of those her trail led, and, crushing far back into the yielding hay, he suddenly found himself at her side. He heard her gasping.

"Go on! Go on! I cannot run another step!"

Terror made him cold. His body lay still. His heart was still, also. Some instinct, from the first, had told him that association with females is dangerous. Now he found himself trapped, and the peril of the hunt swarming in around him!

CHAPTER XIV

Wolf Strategy

THE day freshened every moment. As the light grew stronger, the intricate entanglement of hay drew yellow bars across his vision.

"Go on! Go on!" whispered the panting she-wolf. "Don't wait here with me. We'll both be lost! We'll both be lost!"

He swung his head against her.

"Be still, little fool!" he commanded.

She was still. He could feel that her stifled breathing was choking her. He could feel her shuddering as she strove to control her gasping breath.

He needed that silence to study the approach of danger. The whole hunt had swept down and around the corral. It poured on. He was sure, for a few moments, that it was definitely gone, for there was no noise close at hand except the shrill screeching of the little yellow dog, which had taken up its post directly in front of the hiding place of the two wolves.

That is what comes of foolish mercy to a treacherous

enemy in a time of war, thought Frosty, and all his teeth were on edge with anger and disgust.

Then the hunt came back, as though the yelling of the little dog had guided it. The doors of the house began to slam, and men carrying the deadly odor of gunpowder and steel issued. Their voices were loud. The riders of the hunt had returned. The scent of their sweating horses was strong in the nostrils of Frosty. The great dogs were roving here and there. Chickens, foraging in the early day, fled with scattering outcries from these marauders. And always the cursed dogs were giving tongue.

Had they lost the scent in the entangled mazes of fresh tracks that crossed and recrossed the odorous ground of the corral? Well, the yelping of the little yellow dog would soon lead them aright.

Yes, at this very moment there was a howl from a pointer, and then from another, right at the entrance to the lurking place of the wolves.

Frosty nudged his mate with the shrug of a shoulder. This was the time. By the tightening of his muscles she could be able to judge that a sudden face attack was what he had in mind, and he could feel her muscles tightening, also. There was good stuff in her. She was not one to shrink from her duty in a great pinch like this.

Now came the great voices which Frosty had feared most of all, and waited for—the heavy artillery of the Thurston pack, which was sweeping toward the haystack.

Frosty came out of the hay with a bound. A big pointer, right in front of him, received a slash that opened his shoulder like a knife stroke. That dog would run no more on this day.

The dazzled eyes of Frosty saw men on horseback outside the corral fence. He saw, closer in, greyhounds running, and big, grizzled monsters, covered with mouse-colored, curling tufts of hair exactly like the two dogs of Bill Gary, but even larger, if anything.

The men yelled. The dogs gave tongue all in one voice. And the wretched little yellow dog that had caused all this crisis of danger fled screaming out of the path.

That talkative busybody, the squirrel, betrays many a

84

hiding animal in the heart of the woods. Frosty thought of that as he swerved around the corner of the haystack as fast as he could possibly leg it.

Behind him his fleet-footed mate was racing. The fluff of his tail must be beside her head. And Frosty turned the next corner, and the next of the stack, and bolted straight back across the corral.

He had simply doubled the stack, and was running, now, right on toward the spot where he had seen the horsemen, because he had judged that they would get into motion in another direction.

He was right. They had scattered to this side and to that, and the whole stream of dogs was in movement out of sight, around the big stack of hay, as Frosty and his mate streaked back across the corral and leaped the fence.

A little wilderness of labyrinthine barbed wire crossed and crisscrossed before them, bright with newness and the morning light here, and red with rust there. And Frosty held straight on through the midst of that wire. The strands which were farthest apart he dived between. The lower fences he jumped. He knew of old that ridden horses will not follow across barbed wire, even where it is stretched low along the posts.

Off to the side he saw a little boy and two women at the back of the house, throwing up their hands, yelling in shrill voices. They were not to be considered, however, because no smell of gunpowder and steel came from them.

In fact, Frosty gained so much by his doubling maneuver that he was actually well beyond the entanglements of the corral fencing before the head of the dog pack got wind and sight of him and lurched in pursuit.

The horsemen were coming, too, scattering off to the side to avoid the fences. Rifles began to clang as Frosty shifted into a scattering of brush that worked up a steep hillside. And through that brush the two wolves dodged to the head of the hill.

Frosty glanced at his mate, and saw that she was not scathed. Her eyes were red with labor and with terror. They were blank. She was incapable of using, now, the excellent brain which the god of wolves had put into her

85

head. All that she could do was to follow blindly where her great mate led her.

Her heavy meal of meat still weighted her down, but she was in her second wind. And before them stretched the ragged sea of the mountain uplands which Frosty knew so by heart, every corner, every hole, every den, every patch of brush.

He realized, by the first glimmering of hope, how utterly he had been lost in despair.

He knew the best way to head now. Just off to the right there was a canyon which a small stream of water had drilled and grooved and polished through the rising mountains. If they could get into that ravine they could shift from one side of the narrow water to the other, and so delay the dogs which ran so well by scent. And presently a horde of little branching canyons opened to the right and to the left. Up one of them they could flee and perhaps gain safety.

It only needed that they should first make the long pull of the upgrade that would bring them to the edge of the canyon wall.

He knew the best way, and he showed it to his mate now. There is nothing so killing as an upslope, but wolves handle such labor better than dogs, almost always. He felt that for the moment only man was to be feared, because the light of the day was bright now, and man could use that light to kill from afar with the barking voice of a trusty rifle.

So Frosty legged it up the slope, cut suddenly to the right, and found himself running on an old Indian trail up the side of the valley. Sometimes that trail was ten feet wide. Sometimes it narrowed to three. Would the riders dare to follow on their horses? Or would they give up the hunt and leave it to the dogs to finish the day's work?

The trail rose in a straight line, hugging the great rocky wall of the ravine. From the outer edge of the ancient road the cliff dropped again hundreds of feet to where the little river widened into pools or narrowed again into arrow-straight white rushings of water. It was still a good mile, a long mile, to the place where the trail dipped downward and slipped onto the level floor of the narrow valley. It was still a mile from the broken bad lands where Frosty and his mate could begin to have hope indeed.

And before that mile was over, Frosty knew that he would have to turn and fight.

The pointers had fallen well behind now. They had not the legs to keep up with the arrowy flight of the grey-hounds, and next to the greyhounds came the great fighting dogs of the breed of Bill Gary. The riders were also there, in the distance, driving their horses up the narrow, slippery, dangerous ledge with a remorseless courage. But they could not keep up with the dogs on such a grade as this. Therefore they lost ground at every turn. Only twice did they have a clear view of the fugitives and fill the air with whining bits of lead that made Frosty shift and dodge from side to side.

But the she-wolf was almost spent. Her effort to maintain a gallop sent the loose hide and ruff of her mane swaying forward above her shoulders. Her head was down. Her long red tongue almost brushed the rocks. She ran with a telltale swerving as Frosty suddenly checked, with a snarl that told her to run on.

She went on, but only at a dragging trot. And he, looking after her, realized that it was all the speed she could possibly get out of her exhausted body.

Then he turned to face the danger.

He was in a narrow spot in the trail where it was scarcely a stride broad. Two dogs could come at him at once over this footing. Here they came—the two leading greyhounds, running as evenly as though on a double leash—magnificent thoroughbreds, the pick of the dog pack of Joe Thurston. The length of the race had put them where they belonged—in front. Now, very gamely, they bared their teeth and rushed-in on the wolf. If they could get a toothhold for even a moment, the big fighters of the Gary breed would close and end Frosty's business.

And Frosty knew it. That was why he had no thought at all of his fangs at this moment. He simply stood braced until the last instant, and then he dived for the shoulder of the inside dog. His head was the entering point of the wedge that he drove between that greyhound and the rock way. His shoulder was the heel of the wedge that hurled the tall dog to the side with a resistless impetus that knocked both it and its running mate over the edge of the rock.

Their death yells ran needle-thin through the air and dropped at once into vagueness and distance.

Frosty had no time to waste on triumph. One of the Gary breed was at him now. Frosty went right at his head with a blinding slash of his teeth, and then with a shoulder stroke that hurled him backward, head over heels.

He slipped over the edge of the rock, clung by the fore-legs, slowly, instinctively crawled back to the ledge.

His second in the pack had gone the way of all flesh by that time. Frosty, fighting for life, had cut that big fellow down by the forelegs and rammed him in turn over the edge of the rock.

And now, at last, that best of fighting backs held back. They had seen their leaders, one by one, hurled to destruction. It must have seemed to them that a four-footed devil was standing there, bristling, green fire shooting from his eyes.

So they gave back, howling, snarling. Only the gallant, foolish greyhounds strove to get at the throat of the enemy, but found their way blocked by the massed formation of the Gary dogs, which were now at the front.

So, for a moment, the great wolf stood his ground, and knew that he was giving his mate safe time to cross the top of the ledge and get down into the ravine beneath. And as that knowledge made him glance aside, he saw a thing that curdled his wolfish blood—for, straight across the ravine, lying at ease on the ground, a man was leveling his rifle at Frosty's heart.

CHAPTER XV

Saved by Silver

FROSTY knew that danger as well as though he already felt the bullet in his flesh. There were two men yonder across the ravine, and two horses, one of which shone like a statue of polished gold. The man who lay with the rifle at his shoulder was the vital danger for the moment; his companion was erect, his own rifle held at the ready, and now he leaned and jerked the gun of the marksman aside.

That rifle spoke at the same instant, but the bullet finished far away, and Frosty heard the faint thud of it against the rock high up the cliff. He saw the marksman spring to his feet. He heard the thin, distant voices of dispute blowing toward him.

And even the heart of the wolf knew that it was very strange indeed that men should interfere with one another when it came to the making of a kill.

For his own part, there was a hollow thrill of joy in his heart, and he ran on with lightened body and strengthened legs. Behind him the disheartened pack of dogs had begun to snarl and quarrel with one another. The voices of their owners yelled far away; and so Frosty ran over the peak of the trail and sloped down the farther side into the bottom of the ravine, where his mate was already cantering.

Above him, to the right side of the ravine, he saw the two hunters had mounted. A big man with a bare head rode the golden stallion, and on the bare head of the man there were two faintly gleaming spots of silver, just over the temples, and exactly like the sheen of incipient horns that begin to break out from the head of a deer.

The rough edge of the cliff shut out the view of those two riders for a moment, and Frosty was glad to forget them. The newness of his escape from imminent danger was still a bewilderment in his mind. It was as though his throat had been crushed in the grip of a mighty enemy who, unharmed, had suddenly relented.

But there is no relenting in the wilderness. To slay is to do right, and to destroy the enemy is the first duty.

So when Frosty came to the staggering form of his mate, he looked upon her almost as a visionary thing—a thing that a young cub may daydream or see in the sweeping, tossing spray of a waterfall in summer. She was unreal. The reality remained back there on the trail where the dog pack had confronted him, and where the rifle had pointed at his heart.

He ran up the main ravine, twice springing across the little run of water, leaping from stone to stone that jutted above the surface; and his mate, obediently, though on failing legs, followed him. Then he came to the place where the many smaller ravines split away from the throat of the main valley; and at the same time, far away behind him, he heard the full current of the hunting pack enter the valley.

But he could afford to laugh now. It would take those dogs, no matter how keen, some time to pick up the trail which he had entangled in the lower valley for them. And while they were puzzling over that, he and his mate would be scampering to safety in the labyrinth of canyons that cut up the back country.

He turned, therefore, down the first small ravine to his right.

"A little more," he said to his mate, "and then we rest— we rest!"

She made no answer. She gave no hint that she heard. She ran with slaver falling from her long red tongue. Her eyes seemed swollen; they were closed to mere slits, and showed like unlighted glass. Her coat stood up raggedly, like the coat of a wolf that has been through a frightful winter of famine. Mud and dust covered her. Her heart was breaking, as Frosty very well knew, but where a weaker spirit would have given up and crawled into the first hole, she kept to her work right valiantly. She was the sort of steel of which the right wolfhood should be made, Frosty knew.

He knew, too, that his example and his presence were what finally sustained her during this last effort, and therefore he trotted cheerfully in the front, looking back now and again over his shoulder toward her.

He was looking back in this manner as they rounded a sharp corner of the ravine, and he was surprised to see her stop short.

Was she about to die of weariness, as he had seen a hunted rabbit die?

He glanced ahead, and then he understood!

For there stood the golden stallion with the big rider on his back, and the man was swinging a rope and calling, to his smaller, darker companion:

"We'll take him alive! Don't shoot, Alec!"

Alexander Gary, his rifle leveled from his shoulder, exclaimed in answer: "If you get that wolf on a rope, you'll wish that you'd daubed the rope on the devil, sooner! Lemme put some lead in him. That's the only way to handle him! Let me shoot, Silver!"

"Keep that rifle to yourself!" thundered Silver. "Don't shoot!"

His voice rang and roared through the narrows of the canyon as poor Frosty and his mate halted again, he crowding back to her.

His heart was failing him at last. Before him were two men, reeking with the fatal taint of gunpowder and steel; two men, nearer to him than ever men had been before.

91

And the sun was full and strong upon the scene, and what could keep death from Frosty now?

Then he heard, well in the distance, the cry of the dog pack in the outer valley. In a few moments it would drift in and follow this canyon. There were dogs, and behind the dogs were armed hunters. From that danger there would be no escape, whereas once before these men had pointed a gun at him, and yet he had run to safety.

So, making his choice, Frosty threw his mate one brief, snarling admonition, and started right up the canyon toward the two riders.

The she-wolf lurched after him. She was so far gone that she would have followed the command of Frosty over a precipice blindly. It was all death to her. It had been death almost from the moment that the two pointers began to yell on the trail. It had been death on the run through the hills, death in the hiding of the haystack, death in running through the fencing of the corrals, death in·the agony of long labor up the Indian trail, and now it was doubly death and doubly bitter since, for a moment, there had been a little hope of life.

But she ran heavily after her lord and master.

He was like a lord and master now more than ever before. He had erected his mane. He had thrown his head high. His eyes were balls of green fire as he threatened the two men to this side and to that.

Before him he saw the glimmering on the bright steel barrel of Alec Gary's rifle. The weapon was still at the shoulder of Alec, and he groaned with eagerness as he got, through the sights, a dead bead on the great wolf.

And on the other side of the narrow way, inescapably close, sat the man with the silver gleam in the hair above his temples. He was swinging a rope, opening the noose in it. The thing sang softly in the air. It was thin as a shadow, and it whipped a frail ghost of a shadow over the ground as the rider whirled it.

That was danger, but it was a smaller danger than the rifle. This was that same man, also, who had pulled the rifle away from its line of fire upon the first occasion.

That was why Frosty, compelled to make a choice between dangers, ran much closer to the man with the swinging rope, and as he ran, paid no heed to Jim Silver, but turned all his green-eyed fury, all of his hatred, toward Alec Gary.

And as he came in between the danger of the pair it seemed to Frosty that the hateful steel collar that had been fastened upon him by the will of man now drank up all of the heat of the blazing sun and scalded his neck.

But he was through!

He was through the gap, though the rifle still pointed at him, though the whistle of the swinging rope had been in his very ear.

He was through, and his mate was safely at his heels!

Perhaps they had let him go as a wild cat lets a captured squirrel creep a little way from her terrible claws as she pretends to look the other way, all the while lashing her silken flanks with her tail in an ecstasy of savage exultation, and hate, and rage, and triumph.

Perhaps these men were playing with him and would strike him dead at the moment he thought that he had come to safety.

Alec Gary was groaning: "If you won't let me shoot, then daub the rope on him. There's the steel collar on his neck, and the location of the mine's inside the collar. Jim Silver, are you goin' to let a million dollars of meanness and wolf run right by you?"

"I can't put the rope on him!" exclaimed Silver in answer. "He's too full of nerve. He had plenty of run in him. He could have crawled up the side of one of these rock walls, but he wouldn't leave his mate. He's a hero, Alec. I can't touch him—to-day, I can't!"

Of course Frosty did not understand these words. But what he did understand was that that deep powerful voice was interceding between him and the danger. He knew that out of the throat of Jim Silver was flowing safety for him and for his mate.

Did he feel gratitude?

Well, that was an emotion about which he knew nothing. There is no gratitude in nature—unless it be perhaps between cubs and mothers or such a rare union as that of

93

Frosty and the she-wolf. All that Frosty knew was that a man's voice had given him security. Twice, on a single day, his life had been saved by that same man. Frosty could not attribute motives, but he could understand facts. You may be sure that he was very glad that he had run as close as possible to Silver and as far as possible from Gary!

And behind him, Silver was saying: "I'm sorry, Alec. But I couldn't do it. Not if that collar were worth a million mines. If I'd roped Frosty, we would have had to kill him before we could have quieted him. There was no room to run him and choke him down—not in this narrow ravine. And—man, man, he came right under the noose of my rope. He ran so close to me that it looked as though he were asking me for mercy—trusting me!"

Alec Gary, gray and drawn of face, exhausted by violent emotions, stared at his companion.

"Jim," he said, "everybody knows that you're the best fellow in the world. Everybody understands that. But what's in your head to-day, I can't tell. I thought you and I were hunting a wolf!"

"We are," said Jim Silver contritely. "I've been a fool. We're hunting a cattle-killing devil of a lobo. No matter how big and handsome and brave he is, I'll never be a fool like this again, Alec. Only—something came over me twice to-day. I forgot he was just a wolf. I thought of him just as a brave fellow in danger, in the last ditch."

CHAPTER XVI

Christian's Scheme

THURSTON and his pack of dogs, with Truman, the rancher to back him up, and with the patient and intelligent assistance of Barry Christian and Duff Gregor, kept after Frosty steadily.

In seven days they actually ran the great wolf seven times. They ran Frosty high above timber line over snow and ice; they ran him in the tangles of the canyon that split the lower heights of the Blue Waters. But for a week they had no sight of his mate. Frosty came out alone and faced the hunt and ran it breathless.

There were certain things to notice.

The first day had cost a lot of dog flesh from the pack, but it had afforded a chance to do some shooting at Frosty.

The second day there were three chances to open on Frosty with rifles, and it seemed probable that he had been wounded. The third day they had only a few glimpses of him in the distance. The fourth day they ran the pack by scent only, the greyhounds led behind on leashes to save their valuable and arrowy speed for the right moment. And on that day another dog out of the pack was killed—

a big and wise pointer. The fifth day again they hunted Frosty without sight of his valuable head. They lost another pointer and one of the Gary dogs that day. They lost three of them on the sixth day, and four on the seventh. The very heart had been cut out of Joe Thurston's pack. He had to send back for more dogs.

But he locked his jaw and said that he would keep on along those lines if it took him all summer.

Barry laid his long-fingered hand on the shoulder of Thurston and said in his gentlest voice:

"It won't take you all summer. It won't take you another week. There may be something left of you, but your dogs will all be gone. Look!"

He sat down cross-legged by the camp fire and took out a notebook and began to sketch in it.

"He got the first dogs on the ledge. Call that luck. He was hanging back for his mate, that day, and he just happened to find a place to make a last stand at the very moment that he needed it.

"The second day the dogs were still working him pretty close, but already he had learned to leave the she-wolf behind him. We had a look at him a few times through the sights of our rifles. The third day we had only a glimpse. And since, the dogs have had his scent now and then, and we've had his prints to look at now and then. Not so often, either, because you notice that he prefers to run on hard rock now? The sun burns the scent off rock in a short time, and he knows it. Rock won't take the print of a wolf's paw, and he knows that, too. Every day we work him, we're teaching him how to beat us. The fourth day, he begins to teach us that he knows his lesson. Here, look at this."

He showed the sketch which his rapid pencil had made —a little thicket of brush on a vast, rocky mountainside.

"One of the pointers runs ahead of the rest; and Frosty waits for him and makes the kill, and then goes ahead. See how the kill was made—one long rip right across the throat. Knocked the dog flat with a shoulder stroke first, I suppose. Then Frosty doesn't stay there to exult over the kill. He runs right on and we see no more of him. Neither does the pack.

"The next day, he gets two dogs. He waits for them on the far side of a ford. When the first dog gets across, Frosty pops out of these rocks and slaughters him. While he's killing that one, another of your fighting strength gets across, and Frosty handles him, too. See how it's done. Big dogs—scientific fighters, all of 'em. But Frosty knows how to lay them out. Would you fight a duel with a Frenchman who has been educated all his life to use a sword? That's what it means when any dog gets up against Frosty. Brains, and strength, and teeth that will bite through steel, it seems.

"The next day, you lose three dogs. At different places along the trail. In a dark lane through a patch of big woods—in the narrows of a ravine—in a huge tangle of brush like a jungle. You see, Frosty is beginning to know this pack as well as he knows these mountains. He knows how fast the pack can run and how long it will take him to get to the next cover. He's enjoying the game now. The pack is running after him, but Frosty is doing the hunting.

"Then comes to-day. He leads the pack through the tunnel of a long cave. In the dark he turns around, and two of the best dogs never come out. He takes the pack right back to the ford where he had fought them before, and there he slaughters two more. Notice that every day he grows bolder and bolder, turns to fight more and more often. And yet never lets us get within sight of him."

He finished his sketching and folded his notebook.

Joe Thurston, his coffee cup on his knee, stared at the fire with a small, grim smile, and said nothing.

Truman got up and stretched himself.

"We're beaten," he muttered, under his breath.

Thurston's voice snipped into that sentence sharply.

"You may be beaten. I'm not. Not while the dogs last," he said.

Big Duff Gregor was usually a silent partner in these conversations, only turning his head now and again to wait for wisdom from Barry Christian. But now he ventured:

"It looks like a cooked job. What's the good of wasting our lives? Besides, there may be trouble—"

He let his voice die away, because the sharp glance of Christian had checked him.

Truman, shrugging his shoulders, remarked that he would take a walk through the woods before he turned in, and added that he would start back to his ranch in the morning.

As soon as the rancher was gone, Thurston declared: "You fellows have scared Truman off the trail. That's all right. I don't care if everybody's scared off the trail. I stick to it. What's the trouble that Gregor is afraid of?"

"Gregor believes in luck; he thinks that we've got bad luck permanently on our trail now," put in Christian, before Gregor could speak.

Thurston laughed, and the sound was like the snarling of one of his dogs.

"I know another kind of trouble that you fellows don't want any part of," he said. "Big Jim Silver and a fellow named Gary are still drifting around through the mountains, trying to cut into this game. And you don't want him to sight you. Is that it?"

Christian was rubbing his hands slowly together, nodding, but what he said was:

"Doesn't it occur to you, Thurston, that I may be able to make something out of this wolf hunt that will settle the score between me and Jim Silver? I know that Silver's in this part of the world, but he probably doesn't know that I'm around. Thurston, Truman, and a couple of strangers. That's all he's prepared for. But we'll never bag Jim Silver the way we're going about things now."

Thurston turned his head and waited, his expression poisonously cold.

"Go on, chief," urged Gregor, softening his voice as though he feared to break the current of the thoughts of Christian.

But the great outlaw continued to stare into the distance where the mountains sprang up out of the night and pierced the last color in the sky.

At last he said: "There's a way of doing the thing, I

think. We can get Frosty. We can get Jim Silver, too. But not by tackling either of them directly."

Duff Gregor looked with a quick, small smile toward Thurston, as though he wanted to call Thurston's attention and bid him be ready for an idea that would be worth hearing.

Then Barry Christian said: "Silver trails the wolf, and the wolf trails its mate. We can't catch Frosty by fair means, so we'll catch him by foul. We'll get the she-wolf alive and keep her, then Frosty will have to come to us. Silver will have to come to us, too. We'll have to try to be ready."

He turned his face from the mountains and smiled at the fire, and his eyes glowed. Thurston had jumped up from his place. He glared at Christian for a moment. Then he began to walk up and down with short, quick steps.

"I wish you'd thought of it before," he said. "I'd be in a thousand dollars' worth of dogs, by this time—and maybe we'd have both the wolves drying by the fire."

"It's no easy job to get the she-wolf. She never appears any more," suggested Duff Gregor.

"She'll sure appear to-morrow, though," said Thurston through his teeth.

As a matter of fact, she *did* appear on the morrow. Thurston found an old set of her tracks and worked the dogs down the line to a dugout which was rank with the smell of the wolves. Out of that dugout the pack got the scent of the she-wolf, and though it was crossed and re-crossed by the sign of Frosty, it seemed as though the dogs were glad to forget all about that destroyer. The pack hung closely to the traces of Frosty's mate and, late in the afternoon, suddenly she ran out of cover a mile ahead of the pointers.

Big Frosty was there beside her, but only for a moment; then he disappeared into brush, heading off to the right, while his mate kept straight ahead.

Joe Thurston cursed with hearty amazement, for Frosty's intention of pulling the pack after him while the she-wolf ran free was perfectly apparent.

But on this day, Frosty's luck was out. He had read

human minds very well, indeed, but he could not guess the device which Barry Christian had brought into the game.

Right past the sign of Frosty's diverging trail ran the pack, with the greyhound shooting out into the lead toward the point where the other wolf had disappeared.

There were two burning miles, then the riders brought their foaming horses in view of a big rock under which Frosty's mate had taken her stand, at bay. She had not the foot to distance the greyhounds, of course, and she had not the shiftiness to dodge them, as Frosty would have done.

She had laid one of them writhing on the ground; the others, in a close semicircle, edged in gradually on the raving, green-eyed beauty.

Barry Christian rode right through the dogs and landed the noose of his lariat over her neck just as she whirled to make a break for liberty.

Thurston kept the dogs off. Duff Gregor landed another rope on the big she-wolf. In thirty seconds she was choked to a stagger, muzzled, hobbled, and ready to be dragged wherever her captors wished.

Through the swirl of dust, Thurston looked down at their prize.

"There's the difference between hunting an ordinary wolf and tackling Frosty," he said. "We've got her in one day. We wouldn't get him in one year. Not with an army."

There was a peculiar answer to that speech, for from the opposite side of the valley, unseen among the woods, a wolf gave voice to a great, deep-throated lament; and the three men looked down at the ground with a sudden qualm of shame. They knew it was Frosty mourning for his mate.

CHAPTER XVII

The Hunters' Camp

JIM SILVER lay out on the edge of a bluff with a field glass pressed to his eyes. He studied the opposite slope for a time, then he sat up and passed the glass to Alec Gary.

"Take your turn," he said. "I think it's Frosty's mate. She's chained there. I could see the glitter of the chain."

Gary studied the picture in turn. The powerful glasses picked up the farther mountainside and brought it suddenly closer. It expanded the clearing. He saw the white-headed stump where a tree had been newly felled. He saw the glistening of an ax. And in the middle of a patch of sunset that sloped from the west over the heads of the pines, he made out the big wolf that stalked restlessly up and down. A snaky streak of light coiled and recoiled and followed the captive. That was the chain, of course.

"Looks tall," said Gary. "But I couldn't spot it as Frosty's mate."

"I think so," said Jim Silver. "Dark above and pale below. She sat down while I was watching her, and the breast was almost white. Those are the markings of Frosty's mate. Listen!"

There was a sudden clamor of the voices of dogs. The noise fell away on one yelping sound as though a whip had been used.

"And that's the pack!" suggested Alec Gary.

He lowered the field glasses and shaded his eyes with his hand as though in that manner it would be easier to see the truth. All his lean, dark, handsome face showed the strain.

"That's the pack," he went on. "It's the same lot of people who have been hunting Frosty with the dogs."

"The same lot," said Silver. "Who are they?"

Gary glanced at him and waited. He was always waiting on Silver, as upon the knowledge of a superior being. It was not merely that deference that had caused Silver to feel an affection for him. All during the ardors of that hunt, above timber line and below, through all sorts of weather, the patience and the endurance of Gary had been all that a man could ask for. There seemed to be in him none of the brute that had appeared in his uncle, Bill Gary. In Alec Gary the blood stream had run pure and clear. In every way the work had been difficult, and a dozen times, as they toiled and moiled to make out the trail, they had heard the clamor of the dog pack sweep by in the distance, hurrying miles away, and driving out of their den, once more, the great wolf for whom they hunted. But Gary had never complained.

"I don't know who they might be," said Gary. "Except what I've guessed before—that it's Thurston's pack."

"Tell me," said Silver. "Do you know Thurston?"

"I've seen him. That's about all."

"What sort of reputation?"

"Mean—but straight."

"Really straight? Too straight, say, to throw in with a pair of crooks?"

"What sort of crooks?" asked Alec Gary.

"A crook like Barry Christian, for instance?"

Slowly Gary shook his head.

"No," he said. "Thurston comes of decent people. I've seen his daughter. She's the right stuff. No, I don't think that he'd throw in with Christian. I'm sure he wouldn't.

No decent man would, because everybody knows what Christian is and how he's deviled you."

"Somewhere," mused Jim Silver, "Barry Christian and Gregor are in the mountains on the trail of Frosty. They are unless I'm entirely wrong. Christian knows what's inside that Red Cross collar. And he isn't the sort of a fellow to give up the job until he's put his hands on the treasure."

"Suppose he knew that *you* were after Frosty, too. Would he still keep at the job?" asked Gary.

"He'd keep at the job. He's not afraid of me, if that's what you mean," answered Silver.

"No? Then why does he run away from you?"

"Because he's like a beast of prey. Doesn't fight until he's pretty sure of winning. He wants an advantage before he throws his hat into the ring. But if you think that Thurston wouldn't throw in with Christian—why, then it would be safe enough for you to go over there and find out just who owns that dog pack. Because, Alec, whoever it is will probably have Frosty by the leg before many days."

"You mean," answered Gary, "that they'll cover the ground with traps and that Frosty will walk over those traps to get to his mate?"

"That's what I mean. Has Frosty ever failed to stand by her, so far?"

"No," agreed Alec Gary. "He's a regular lion when it comes to standing up for her."

"He'll keep away for a while, perhaps. And when he comes in, first of all, he'll smell the traps and clear off. But finally he'll close his eyes and take a chance. It will be the last chance that he ever takes."

Gary nodded.

"And that," said Silver, "will be the end of the trail. The people who catch the wolf will be sure to examine the collar he's wearing. They'll open the little compartment. They'll find the message about the mine. They'll get the fortune that ought to be yours, Alec, and you'll have all of this work for nothing."

Gary squinted at the distance, a way that all mountain men have when they are in earnest thought.

"Not for nothing," he answered. "I've learned to know you, Jim. That's enough for me."

Silver smiled at him. "Ride down there and take a look at the camp, will you?" he asked. "You can be back here before the twilight's very deep. You haven't pulled the saddle off your horse yet, and Parade has started grazing already."

The stallion, hearing his name, tossed up his head and looked anxiously toward his master, scented the wind, made sure that all was well on all sides, and resumed his grazing.

"I'll have the camp made and the fire started," said Silver. "I'll have the meat cooked before you get back."

"I'll be here again before dark," agreed Gary. "And we ought to know who those people are. Jim, you really think that they'll get Frosty?"

"They will," said Silver. "We're as good as beaten now. They had the brains to tackle the problem on its easier side. I never thought of doing that."

Gary sighed. But without making the least complaint, he swung into the saddle and rode off down the hillside.

Silver watched him for a short time. The way led steeply down into the valley and then up through a thickness of pines toward the clearing. Already the clearing was lost in thick shadows as the sun dropped lower in the west.

It was the moment of the day which Silver liked best of all, next to the pure, still colors of the dawn. If he had been alone, he would have stood motionless, watching the day end and the fires of it soak out into the dim vapors of the night, but Gary was not accustomed to living like a wild Indian, and needed at least two good meals a day, with three preferred.

So Silver, with a sigh, turned to the cookery.

He could not help wishing to find, one day, a man like himself, capable of enjoying life even if there were only one meal a day—yes, or once in two days, if necessary— a man with all of his appetites perfectly under control, except that passionate and urgent appetite for the wilderness. He had never found a man of that sort. He was reasonably sure that he never *would* find one. In the whole

104

course of his life he had found one living creature that he felt was like himself—and that was the great stallion, Parade. He did not own Parade. He had simply formed a partnership with the horse. Of men, there was of course Taxi—but Taxi was not a blood brother. Whatever the affection between them might be, they were total opposites.

These were the rather gloomy thoughts of Jim Silver as he broke up some wood for the camp fire, and cut a number of small twigs to serve as spits for the rabbit meat. Young Alec Gary, with an accurate rifle, had picked off two jack rabbits that afternoon. They had been partially dressed, immediately after the killing, of course. Now Silver finished the cutting up of the meat and arranged it on the spits around the handful of flame.

That, and salt and cold water, would be their fare. And perhaps a few bits of hard-tack. Ample for Silver, but starvation diet for Gary, as Silver well knew.

Parade posted himself to windward of the fire and close in toward it.

At a greater distance he would find far better grazing, free from the brush, but Parade always chose the strategic position rather than the one where he could fill his stomach most easily. Now, as he grazed, whether his head was down or up, he would be continually on guard. And even when he lay down to sleep, his senses would not be totally closed. His nostrils would still be drinking the wind and sifting the messages that were borne on it to his subconscious brain. His keen ears would be listening for the sound of feet or of distant voices. And, at the first token of peril, he would be up and snort and stamp beside his master until Jim Silver wakened.

He made a better sentinel than a dozen trained men, and Silver trusted the horse more in dangerous country. Though, for that matter, all country was dangerous where Jim Silver rode. His friends made much noise, but they were always at a distance. His enemies were apt to be on his trail.

He was thinking of these things, more gloomily than ever, when he was aware that the twilight had ended. The meat he had been turning on the spits was now browned

105

and ready for eating. He wrapped that meat in some clean leaves, stood up, and cast one guilty glance toward the stars. He felt that he had been asleep at his post, indulging in useless reflections.

For well before this, his friend should have returned.

He went to the brow of the hill overlooking the deep valley, and stared in the direction of the clearing. It was invisible now. The trees seemed to march in unbroken ranks up the opposite steep slope. Only on the ridge they bristled against the dim background of the starlight.

There Silver waited, watching, listening.

The fact that there was no firelight from the opposite clearing was suspicious enough, for people were still there. At least, the dogs were there. Even now Silver heard a short, eager yelping that floated faintly to him on the thin mountain air.

Danger was in that air, and he knew that he would have to go straight on to investigate the source of it. He saddled Parade and rode at once into the deeper night of the valley.

CHAPTER XVIII

Bait for Silver

THE day is always two or three hours shorter under a heavy growth of pine trees. The morning light needs time to soak down through the branches, as it were; and in the evening the night seems to rise up out of the ground.

So it seemed to young Alec Gary as he rode his mustang up the mountainside toward the clearing. It was already twilight in those woods. But there was still a dull rosy golden light in the air when he came out into the open.

Before him he saw the big she-wolf. At his coming she had slunk to the other end of her chain and cowered against the ground, her bright eyes flashing from side to side as she vainly searched for some means of escape.

On the far side of the clearing there was a straight face of rock some twenty-five or thirty feet high. He had not been able to see it from across the valley, no doubt because of the way the shadows from the trees fell across the polished face of it. Off to the side, half lost among the trees, he could see the shadowy forms of the leashed dogs. But more interesting than anything else, to the eye of Alec

Gary, was the slender figure of Joe Thurston standing facing him with a loaded rifle.

"Hello, Thurston," he said. "You don't have to shoot. I'm a friend."

He laughed a little, as he said this.

"You're a friend, are you?" said Thurston. "And what makes you think that I expect to see any enemies around here?"

"The point is that I *don't* think it," answered Alec Gary. "But you seem to be ready for anything."

"That's a good way to seem," answered Thurston.

His thin lips kept twisting a little, and his eyes were always focusing and narrowing as though he were picking out the part of Gary's body into which he intended to put a slug of lead.

He added: "What brought you up here, and who are you?"

"Alec Gary. I'm up here with a friend of mine."

"Alec Gary? I don't remember that name. Ever see me before?"

"Yes. I remember you, all right. But I'm not important enough to be looked at twice."

This modest remark brought no smile from Thurston.

"It's a funny time to be breaking in on a camp, seems to me," he said. "If you've got a friend with you, where is he?"

"Back yonder," said Gary, with a very general wave of his hand.

"Back where?"

"Over yonder."

"Who is he?" asked Thurston. "Don't beat around the bush like this. Who is he?"

"A fellow you may have heard of. His name is Jim Silver."

The effect was instant. Thurston dropped the butt of his rifle to the ground and nodded.

"Jim Silver's with you, eh?" he said. "And doing what? Hunting Frosty?"

"How do you guess that?"

"Silver can't do anything that people won't talk about,"

said Thurston. "Every time he lifts his hand, the shadow falls right across the sky." He chuckled, amused by his own conceit.

"Get off your horse and sit down," said Thurston finally. Gary accepted the invitation.

"There's nothing cooked yet," said Thurston. "Can't offer you anything."

"That's all right. Other fellows out hunting grub?"

"What other fellows?" snapped Thurston.

"Why," said Gary, "you couldn't be up here handling and feeding a mob of dogs like this all by yourself."

But he was disturbed by the sudden way in which Thurston had snapped the words at him.

"I can handle those dogs and more," was all that Thurston replied.

"That's Frosty's mate, isn't she?" asked Gary.

"What makes you think so?"

"Why else would you have her on a chain?"

"Because she's the finest she-wolf that I've ever seen. Some of the museums are always looking for outstanding specimens like her. They get plenty of fine dog-wolf pelts for stuffing, but mighty few females that are not runts."

Gary merely smiled.

"You don't believe me, eh?" asked Thurston, frowning.

"Sure, that's all right," answered Gary. "I believe anything that you want to tell me."

"Thanks," said Thurston coldly.

He kept on eying Gary as though with a profound distrust.

"All right," said Gary. "You don't have to open up and talk. We're both after the same scalp, and I suppose you'll get it—now that you have this museum hide staked out. Do you always do that, Thurston?"

"Do I always do what?"

"Stake out your big wolves and cool 'em off with a little walking on a chain before you take their hides?"

Joe Thurston snapped suddenly: "You're too curious."

"Sorry," said Alec Gary slowly.

Thurston turned suddenly on his heel and walked off through the trees.

He simply tossed over his shoulder the words: "He's Jim Silver's hunting partner, and Silver is somewhere around here."

Whom was he addressing? Alec Gary glanced over his shoulder and saw two big men stepping out from behind the pine trees. One was heavily, strongly made about the shoulders and narrow through the hips; in body and in face he was something of the appearance of Jim Silver, though he was less clean-cut. His companion had a rather long, pale, handsome face. He looked as though he had not been much in the sunlight. His hair was very long. He had supple hands with very long fingers. One might have expected to see him sitting at an easel pointing a woodland scene rather than drawing a revolver with a practiced ease.

"Who are you, partner?" he asked as he approached.

His voice was wonderfully soft, gentle and low but that did not seem an excellent thing to Alec Gary. He had heard a cat purr on much the same note. In the face of the pale man's companion there was a frank and open glint of mockery.

"My name is Alec Gary," he answered. "Who are you?"

"Wilkins," said the stranger. "This is my partner, Hal Murphy."

"Or Jones?" queried Alec Gary. "Or Smith? Or Brown?"

For the falsity of the name suddenly rang hollow on his ear. He regretted that he had allowed his tongue to take the mastery over him.

"Wilkins" continued to regard him with a quiet eye.

"You're with Silver, are you?" he asked.

"I'm with Jim Silver," answered Gary, reassured as he mentioned the name.

For, even if these fellows were outlaws, they would be certain to respect that famous and terrible name.

"Then," said the pale-faced man, "perhaps you wouldn't mind spending a little time with us?"

"Why should I?" asked Gary.

"Because," said the other, while his companion suddenly grinned more broadly, "Jim Silver knows me, and when he comes looking for you, to-night, I want him to find me in."

"Jim Silver knows you?" repeated Gary. He could understand that there was a threat in the air, but he could not make out what seemed a very twisted meaning.

The pale man kept smiling gently at him. His voice was more poisonously caressing than ever as he answered: "You see the she-wolf, Gary?"

"Well?" asked Gary.

"She's bait for Frosty. She's his mate."

"I guessed at that," answered Gary, frowning.

"And I've been hoping," said the other, "that Jim Silver might come investigating at about the same time that Frosty dropped in on us. But now that you've decided to stay with us, I'll be the surer that Silver will come. Because there is one thing that one can always be sure of, when Jim Silver is in the case. He won't let his friends down. Never! If one of 'em gets in a pinch, honest Jim Silver, brave Jim Silver, noble Jim Silver will never fail to put his head in the lion's mouth to get the fellow out of trouble."

A strong chill of dread passed through Alec Gary, body and mind.

"What trouble?" he asked. "I don't follow you!"

"Don't you? Be patient, brother, be patient. If you stay here with us, you see, Jim Silver might get a wrong idea in his head. He might think that you were being forced to stay. He might think that we'd drawn guns on you, and tied you hand and foot, and that we intended to keep you until we decided how we'd cut your throat. And ideas like that are just the things to bring out all the nobility of Mr. Silver. Oh, I could tell you some strange stories about the ways he has walked into danger for the sake of his friends. Eh?"

The silent companion nodded and grinned. Both of them were watching Gary steadily, and a big Colt kept shifting in the supple hand of the pale man.

"Who are you?" broke out Gary suddenly.

"Why," said the pale man, "as you suggested a while ago, you might call us Smith, or Jones, or Brown, or, perhaps, Barry Christian and Duff Gregor!"

At this, as the flesh of Gary turned to stone, Gregor broke out:

"Why give him the names, Barry? That's a fool play, it seems to me!"

"Because," said Christian calmly, "after he's been used, he won't be alive to talk about us, Duff."

He made a gesture that jerked up the muzzle of the Colt.

"Put up your hands, you poor half-wit," he said to Gary. "You've walked right in on us, and now you'll stay a while."

There was plenty of fighting blood in Alec Gary. To put up his hands meant to surrender his hope of living. But not to raise them, as he plainly saw in the face of Barry Christian, meant to die at once. Besides, the evil name of the man enchanted him and killed his heart. Slowly he raised his hands in surrender.

CHAPTER XIX

The Coming Storm

JIM SILVER, as he went down the hillside on Parade, heard out of the north and the west a heavy rumbling, as if a great wagon were rolling over a wooden bridge, gradually disappearing.

The noise died away. It began again. Then he saw the glimmer of distant lightning above the mountaintops. Either that was a storm which would presently walk up across the sky and put out the stars, or else it was to be confined to the farther side of the range, only its head showing in thin flashes above the crest of the peaks.

He passed the bottom of the valley, and Parade started through the trees, weaving suddenly to this side and then to that, for Parade knew perfectly well that branches which he could easily clear himself might nevertheless sweep his master out of the saddle, and when Silver was on his back, the man was a part of the horse. One nervous system seemed adequate for them both. So they went snaking through the woods at a pace that would have been ruinous for any other rider on any other mount.

When they were well up the slope of the mountain, at

about the place where Silver expected to find the clearing, he halted Parade, dismounted, and whispered for a moment into the ear of the great horse. Parade would stand quietly now, straining his ears to hear from his master even the faintest and most distant whistle. And if there were a sound of footfalls coming toward him through the woods, Parade could tell perfectly if the step of his master were among the noises. Otherwise he would shift and give ground and hide himself with all the cunning of some great jungle beast.

So Silver left him and went gradually forward, listening continually for noises of any sort. Now and again he heard the voices of the dogs as they whimpered in their sleep or wakened to growl at imaginations of the night.

That was all that he could make out until he suddenly found himself clear of the trees. That was all he could make out for an instant, but dropping to one knee, he commenced to scan everything around him with care until the starlight showed him the main details.

He was on the verge of the clearing. Yonder skulked the she-wolf, with the long steel chain clinking musically as she walked back and forth. Now she lay down and gritted at the chain with her strong teeth; and out of the distance—no, it was not so very far away—Frosty's melancholy call came echoing through the woods.

Then a man's voice said: "He's on the trail now. He's pretty close, too."

The words were not what made Silver flatten himself against a tree to gain a better shelter. They were not what brought the Colt suddenly into his hand. But it was the voice that ran all through him with an electric shock of savage joy and desire.

It was the prime goal of all his questing, and he was now in reaching distance of it. It was Barry Christian who spoke there.

He could see the man, at first obscured against the shadow of the trees, but now discernible with a smaller companion at his side. Whoever it was, it was not Duff Gregor.

"He's coming in," said the smaller man. "I thought he'd

have more sense. It's a pity in a way, Barry. It's like seeing a great man throw himself away on account of a woman."

"I'll pity him to-morrow, if I can catch him to-night," answered Christian. "Whisper hears him now. Listen to her whining."

"Who gave her that name?" asked the smaller man.

"Gregor," said Barry Christian. "And it fits her. If it weren't for the chain that she carries around, we'd never hear her moving."

"Whisper!" said the other. "Well, isn't it time for you to get on guard? Isn't Silver likely to show up any moment?"

"Not for a time, I think," said Christian. "Only the devil can tell just what Silver will do or how long it will take him to do it. But he won't be here for a while, I suppose. If he does come—well, he may simply blunder into the clearing and—"

His voice stopped.

"You'll have only starlight to shoot by," said the smaller man.

"There are handfuls of buckshot in those shotguns," said Christian. "We won't miss. This time of all times, we won't miss."

They retired toward the base of the big rock. From the darkness there, unseen, the voice of Alec Gary spoke. There was the hard, smacking sound of a blow and a snarling answer. Gary spoke no more. One of the dogs whimpered, as though in sympathy. Then the forest settled back into silence.

It was only silence close at hand. In the distance there was still the muttering and the rumbling of the thunder, from time to time.

Silver remained on one knee. If ever he had been close to praying, he was close now; and if ever temptation had taken him by the throat, it had been when the dark form of Barry Christian loomed so close through the night. One flick of Silver's thumb over the hammer of his revolver, and Barry Christian would have gone, at last, to his final account. It seemed to Jim Silver, as he kneeled there, that there was a perverse deity controlling him, bringing him

115

so often close to the great criminal, and so often letting Christian slip away from him again.

He had lodged Christian in prison, to await the death penalty; and Christian had managed to escape almost on the last day. He had seen Christian hurled into a flooded river that ran like a galloping horse toward a cataract. But chance and the unlucky hands of another man had drawn Christian out of the danger that time. And now, as Silver kneeled in the dark, he knew that at last he could bring the trail to an end and kill his man. It was the thing for which he had waited. It was an incredible good fortune that had brought Christian into his hand. He would speak one word—and then the bullet would strike.

But the thought of young Alec Gary held Silver back. Gary was somewhere near. Gary and a she-wolf were baits for him and for the great wolf, Frosty.

That thought was still working in his mind, holding his hand, as Christian moved away through the darkness. And then, after Gary had spoken and had been silenced, and after the dog had whimpered and silence fallen yet again, Silver was aware that something lived beside him. There had been no sound of the approach, but something was there—something formidably big and dangerous.

Gradually he turned his head and saw, hardly two steps away, the dim loom of the figure of a wolf.

Perhaps it was because Silver was on one knee, but it seemed to him at the first glance that the creature had the outline of a wolf but the bulk of a bear. A shock of fear struck Silver.

Then he realized that it was Frosty.

He had come through the darkness to the edge of the clearing. Would he venture out across ground that was doubtless sewed thick with traps?

The big fellow drifted a little forward, crouched on his belly, stretched out a shadowy paw, and then drew it back. He moved to the side, and then the wind seemed to come to him from the man so close.

There was an instant of pause. Frosty bristled to his full height. The green glare of his eyes burned into the soul of Silver. And then he was gone. For all the speed

116

of that withdrawal, still there had not been a sound.

Was that not another of the ironies which chance was heaping upon the head of Jim Silver on this night? The wolf had been there beside him. He had even been able to make out the glimmer of the steel links of the collar that was around his neck. And yet Silver had not dared to shoot.

He had not dared because of Alec Gary. The young fellow seemed to be hung like a leaden weight around his neck.

But what could be done?

To cross the clearing was impossible because of the traps. It was impossible because of the shotguns, also. For Barry Christian would not miss. Even Silver himself was hardly a hairbreadth more accurate with weapons than Christian—and on this night Christian would be shooting for the prize of all his life.

How to come at the prisoner at the base of the rock, then?

It was typical of Christian that he should have had wit enough to secure his man at a point which was so perfectly open, and which was nevertheless so unapproachable.

Suppose that Silver tried to skirt around through the woods and come at the others?

Well, there would be traps through the woods, too— on the verge of them, at least. And if a wolf trap closed on his foot it would be a bad business—the last business for Jim Silver in this world.

He gritted his teeth and waited for a thought. None came.

He withdrew through the trees to Parade and saw the pale glimmer of the great eyes of the horse. Parade stood with high head, turning it a little from side to side, his ears stiffly forward as he listened and scented a hundred dangers. His fear was so great that he had broken into a fine sweat, but still he waited at his post for his master. And a great outrush of admiration for the dumb brute poured from the heart of Silver. What is so admirable as those who can endure even when they cannot understand?

As he stroked the horse, his hand touched the rope

117

which was coiled and tied to the front of the saddle. With it came his first hope of making the delivery of Alec Gary.

It was only a vague hope, for the scheme seemed so ridiculous that he smiled and shook his head in the darkness. He gripped his hands hard, also, and flexed the big muscles of his arms.

He was stronger, far stronger than other men, and yet he could not help doubting the sufficiency of his might for the task which he contemplated.

He took Parade back through the woods, circled them at a distance, and as the wind blew from him toward the clearing, he heard the dogs of the pack break out into one of their sudden clamors. He continued in the wide sweep of the semicircle, quitted Parade in the trees up the slope, and at last came slowly forward, carrying the rope which he had taken from the saddle.

He had laid his course, through the darkness of the night and the trees, with such accuracy that he came out just above the lip of the rock at the foot of which the men of the camp were posted.

The night was dimmer than ever. It seemed that the storm which had been roaring in the north and west was now breaking out of the higher mountains and approaching this section. Gusts of wind moaned distantly through the trees or sounded close at hand with sudden rushings. Big clouds, also, were poured in broken streams across the sky, so that the stars were blotted out in great parts of the heavens. But in intervals of the noise of the coming storm, Silver, stretched out at full length on the ground, staring down from the ledge, could hear and vaguely see the men below.

CHAPTER XX

Rope Rescue

WHAT Silver made out, at last, was one figure continually in place at the bottom of the rock. That he took to be his friend, particularly since the silhouette never moved, and therefore was probably bound hand and foot. There were three others who changed places from time to time. Sometimes one of them would move away into the woods on one side, and sometimes one would pass into the other trees. He heard the name "Thurston" used, which served to identify the smaller man of the trio. The others would be Christian and Gregor, of course.

As his eyes grew more used to the broken starlight, he could make out the details more clearly. Above all, he could see the double-barreled shotguns whose big charges of buckshot could be sent home without much light to aim by. Sometimes all three of the men on watch were pooled together for a few moments, and on those occasions there was most of the talk that he was able to hear. The voices were kept low, but the face of the rock was hollowed and curved in such a way that it gathered the noises like a sounding board.

At one of those times, Silver heard Thurston say: "This may be a rotten business. People are going to ask a lot of questions if Jim Silver disappears. The other one, here— I don't suppose that he'll count so much."

"People won't have any questions to ask. Not for years," said Christian. "No one is likely to show up in this neck of the woods for a long time. We're pretty far back in the tall timber, you know. The main thing is to realize that Silver often disappears for months at a time. Every one realizes that."

"What does he do when he disappears?" asked Thurston.

"Nobody knows. Some people say that he has a mine staked out somewhere, and when he runs out of funds, he goes back to the place and grinds up more ore in his coffee mill and washes out some more dust," said Christian.

"What does he need money for, when he lives worse than a wild Indian most of the time?" asked Thurston.

"He needs it to throw away," said Christian. "The fool can't keep money in his pocket. Any fellow with half a brain about him can wheedle every penny out of the hand of Jim Silver. But I don't think he spends his lost time at any mine."

"Why not?"

"Because it would be beneath him. That's one of his poses. Pretends to despise gold and everything that it will do. He probably just goes out into the woods and gets close to nature."

"How close?"

"Well, he can whistle like any bird you name; he can chatter like a squirrel and hoot like an owl and growl like a bear. He knows the look of every tree and blade of grass. That's why he knows how to follow a trail. He can almost see in the dark."

"I hope not," said Thurston. "That might be bad business for us."

Christian merely laughed.

"Not so bad," he said. "He won't shoot you in the back, no matter what happens. There's no Indian in him. He'll give you as much warning as a rattlesnake before he starts spraying lead."

That was the brief picture of Silver that Christian painted, and as it ended, Thurston asked:

"Why does he hate you, Christian? What good would it do him to nail you down?"

"Newspaper space," said Christian. "He wants glory. And he thinks that there isn't room enough in the world for the two of us."

"Well," said Thurston, "if he's as clever as you say, and can work in the dark so well, it's pretty certain that he won't run into the trap that you've laid for him."

"It doesn't matter what he sees," answered Christian. "The fool has a sort of a code that he lives by. If he has a partner, he has to get the other fellow out of trouble every time. He knows that if we have young Gary, we'll make a dead man of him by the time the day commences. Sometime before the dawn, he's sure to try his hand. He may do anything he can think of that's clever, but cleverness won't help him now. There's only one way for him, and that's to rush the camp!"

"Aye," exclaimed Gregor, exultantly, "and that will mean one Colt against three shotguns. But can't he work some trick here?"

"Look around for yourself," said Christian. "What can he do? If he had wings, he might drop down out of the air and carry Gary off in his talons. That's about all that he could manage, I take it."

Then he commanded: "Keep on the stir. The best way to handle him is to meet him on the way and get in the first shot. He'll sneak up through the trees probably, on one side or the other. Keep sifting in and out. Use your eyes and use your ears. This storm that's blowing up makes everything a lot harder for us."

The trio broke up again. Thurston and Gregor moved off to the trees, and Christian remained walking up and down in front of the prisoner.

The sky was now almost totally covered with clouds. The stars whirled through the rents, now and again. The wind struck in quickening gusts, with a louder roaring, and when the lightning played in the northwest, it showed a hood of rain lowered over the higher mountains. Sometimes the lightning seemed to set all the rain on fire, like a gas, and against that dull flare the big trees stood out. There was one thunder-blasted giant with a half-naked head that remained seared forever upon the memory of Jim Silver.

Rain began to rattle around him, big drops that splashed from the polished rock against his face in fine spray. The weight and sting of the drops he could feel against the back of his neck. He had taken off his hat. The wind cuffed his head from behind and pulled almost painfully at the roots of his hair.

He was cold, he was wet, but he remained in his place, motionless, watchful as a cat beside a mouse hole.

Then, at last, he had his chance.

All three of the watchers had, for the moment, stepped out of sight. Rain was falling in sheets now. It would ease away in a moment, he felt sure. But the lightning flash that fell jagged out of the heart of the sky just overhead showed him the polished, wet green of the trees, the cowering she-wolf in the clearing, the bowed form of the captive, and not even a glimmer of any of the guards. They were effectively carrying out Barry Christian's doctrine of watching in the trees for the approach of the rescuer.

Instantly he dropped the noose of his rope—and missed the figure below him!

He jerked up on the rope and got nothing. The wind must have blown the noose awry to spoil his cast.

He tried again, though in a misty darkness that shut out view of his target. Through the smother of the rain he cast with a wider noose, and hauled in, and again he caught nothing.

The rain, instead of letting up, fell now with a mightier violence than ever. It struck on his back with ten million little hammer beats. Then the lightning cleaved the watery air again and showed him a scene covered with dark or glistening pencil strokes of rain, like a photograph taken in a dim room. He could see the target, that instant, and as he threw the noose of the rope again, he saw something else—a vaguely outlined figure not far away, coming out from the trees. The man was Gregor, walking with his shotgun sheltered under his arm, his head down to the rush of the rainfall.

The thunder burst over the head of Silver like a load of rocks on a tin roof. He pulled in on the rope, half despairingly. He could not believe his fortune when he found a weight attached to it!

He rose to his feet. Already, long before, he had selected the small jags of rock on which he would brace his feet. He planted himself accordingly and hauled. He had feared that it was merely an outthrust of rock at the base of the cliff that he might have snared, but he found a ponderous, loose weight at the bottom of his line.

He could not get a free haul on the weight. He had to lean back to get his full strength at the work, and that meant that the rope ground against the edge of the cliff, and the friction used up a large part of his effort.

He took short arm hauls, giving himself half a second of rest between the efforts, his right fist braked against his hip. The weight grew heavier and heavier, or so it seemed.

He prayed that there might not be another flash of lightning. In the extremity of his labor, his head jerked back with each swing of his body, and that was how he saw the clouds breaking above him, the stars showing through like a whirl of bright golden bees.

The weight came closer. He could tell that by the shorter oscillations of the rope. Then the greatest of his efforts failed to budge the rope.

Fear made his eyes swell suddenly in his head. He took a breath, made ready, and hauled with all his might.

There was not the slightest give!

Had the body or the clothes of Gary caught against a sharp projection of the rock? He leaned and made the free end of the rope fast to a knob of rock. As he finished the knot, the rope slacked out a little. And then, again, the lightning split the heavens, and the thunder shouted at his ear, filled his brain with deafness.

Not total deafness, however, for as he crawled to the

side of the ledge, he heard a wild voice, the voice of Gregor, shouting from below:

"Silver's here! Silver! He's hauling Gary—"

Before the words ended, a shotgun roared, and a whistling blast of the buckshot tore the air just in front of Silver. If he had leaned out from the rock an instant sooner, that discharge would have knocked out his brains, he knew.

As it was, he found that his first guess had been right. It was a projecting rock that had halted the upward progress of Gary. It was, in fact, the very edge of the cliff itself! He groaned at his folly in not calculating, accurately, just how much slack he would have to draw in to bring the body to the lip of the rock, for here was the prisoner, pressed close against the ledge, in easy arm reach.

Silver gripped the other's coat at the nape of the neck with a mighty hand and lifted until the springing tendons on his back and shoulder threatened to snap—but he managed to sway Gary up and over the ledge.

They sprawled flat, side by side, as two more shotguns belched in the lower darkness, and the terrible, ringing voice of Christian began to shout revilings at Gregor.

"The horses!" shouted Christian. "Get the horses! We'll cut 'em off in the woods. This is going to be our night before it finishes!"

Silver, with one hand, drew his hunting knife to cut the bonds of Gary. With the other hand he fumbled at the ropes. And the first thing that he found was that his lariat was around the head of the captive! In his effort to free the man, had he hanged him?

He removed the noose, cut the bonds, tore the gag from the mouth of Gary, and jerked him to his feet. A loose figure sagged against him. A dead, limp weight remained in his arms.

CHAPTER XXI

The Trap Is Sprung

LIGHTNING played again. By the thrusting flash of it, Silver saw the face of his friend. It looked like death, and horrible death. The mouth sagged wide open, and there was blood about the corner of it. The rope mark was pressed into the flesh still, as though Gary had bitten at the rope and tried to keep it in place in that manner, when he first felt the noose slipping up around his body after the last cast of Silver. The earlier casts must have brushed him and warned him of the manner in which his friend was fishing to save his life from above.

Perhaps the pressure of the rope alone had been enough to strangle Gary. Perhaps the effect of the gag which had been wedged inside the teeth of Gary plus the rope had turned the trick.

Silver moved the body. The head fell limply back. The eyes were partly open. Another flare of the lightning showed that.

He stood there with a helpless bulk in his arms—and terrible Barry Christian and his men were coming on horses to comb the woods for prey!

Silver threw the body of Alec over his shoulder and ran stumblingly back to Parade. Over the withers of the horse he bent the burden, mounted, and made the loose hulk sit up before him.

Now he was ready for flight, at least, if Christian should sight him. And at the same time he heard what was a sweet music to his ears—a faint, gasping sound from the throat of Alec Gary.

Silver instinctively threw upward one look of gratitude. Then he sent Parade swiftly through the darkness down the slope. It might be that he would encounter the enemy on either one side of the way or the other, but he took the chance because already another idea had come to his mind.

Alec Gary was fighting hard for breath now, groaning and gasping, and life was returning rapidly into his inert body. He was able to maintain himself erect by the time Silver had circled back through the woods to the point which he desired.

Then from the mountain slope just above, he heard the crackling of guns, a brief burst, silence, a distant shouting.

Had they mistaken one another in the darkness, and opened fire blindly? Silver could not help smiling as he thought of that possibility. He was out of the saddle. Gary had slid down to the ground, still gasping for breath.

"Stay here—move if the horse wants to move," Silver warned him, and glided straight ahead toward the clearing.

Lightning showed it to him through the trees. He saw the open space and the chained she-wolf. Straight to her he went. She lay flat, as though to be exposed to the lightning without any shelter over her head had left her senseless.

In one moment the flying fingers of Jim Silver had loosed the collar from her neck. As he stood up, he heard a faint whine that diminished along the ground. And the mate of Frosty was gone like a streak away from his feet.

With her went the nearest chance of capturing Frosty and the secret of the lost gold mine. But at least she had been taken from the hands of Christian; she would no longer serve as a lure to drag back the great Frosty into a trap.

Silver rejoined Gary.

What he wanted, and what he hoped, was to find Gary sufficiently well to take care of himself; instead, he discovered Gary lying on the ground, softly groaning. And that ended his chance of taking Barry Christian and Gregor and Thurston in hand that night. His duty would be to Gary first. Once more the heir of Bill Gary was a load tied to his neck.

So he got Gary back on Parade and rode behind him down the slope of the valley and up the farther side.

He regained the old camping ground. He could trust that Barry Christian would hardly hunt for him that far afield, to find him with his helpless man. Therefore he ventured on building a fire well screened about by rocks and trees so that the only strength of it rose straight upward in the air. He stretched his sick man by that fire and covered him with a slicker. Gradually the warmth restored the tied-up circulation of Gary, though still for a long time every breath he drew was a muffled groan.

When he could speak, he said: "They would have murdered me by morning. They would have done me in. I heard Christian say so."

"I heard the same thing," said Silver. "But they missed you—forget about it!"

"Forget about hell and the chief devil on the job!" muttered Gary. He stared at the fire with great eyes, and then rubbed his battered, torn mouth. He spat blood. His whole body was trembling.

"I felt the rope brush me two or three times," he said. "If I could have moved, I would have rolled away. If I could have yelled, I would have called for help. I began to strangle with fear. I had a crazy idea in my head that I must be blocking the entrance to some snake's den, and that some big, poisonous rattler was about to sock his fangs into me. It didn't occur to me that a rattler would have sounded off first. And then the rope caught around me. I understood then. I knew that you were up there fishing for me, Jim. But I didn't see how it could work. I didn't see how you'd have strength to pull me up."

127

"I was a half-wit," said Silver. "Otherwise I would have brought up Parade and hitched the rope to him. I would have hauled you up with Parade instead of with my arms."

He paused. Gary nodded. Then he went on:

"Then I felt the cursed noose slipping up around me little by little. It wouldn't catch hold around my body. It wouldn't catch me around the shoulders. When it slipped off my shoulders, I leaned my head forward. My mouth was held gaping—wide open—by the gag that Gregor had shoved into it. I couldn't bite on the rope, but I could hook my teeth over it. Then came a big strong pull that lifted me right off the ground. The noose froze in on my head. The ring of it ground into the base of my skull. I thought it was smashing the bone. The fore part of it crushed back into my mouth. I thought I'd be strangled, or that my head would smash in.

"I tried to get the rope out of my mouth. It seemed better to die the way Christian would kill me than the way I was dying then. But I couldn't get the rope out of my mouth. The noose was freezing into me deeper and deeper. It shoved the gag back into my mouth until I couldn't breathe any more. I was strangling. All the time I was being hauled up higher and higher, and all the time the noose was biting into me, constricting, tearing at the flesh, threatening to smash in my skull. But the strangling was the worst. There was blackness with spinning red lights across it. Then there was just the blackness and no lights at all. And after that—I died. I mean I thought it was death. It was just the same as death. Just the same agony.

"But afterward I saw the whirled lights and the blackness. I was on Parade, and your hands were holding me up."

He had talked himself back into a full realization of life, and how near he had come to losing it. Now he sat up suddenly and stared at Silver.

"Nobody else would have thought of that," he said. He measured the heavy shoulders of Silver with his eyes. "And nobody else would have had the strength to do it, even if he had thought about the trick. But if I can get my chance at Barry Christian and Gregor, maybe I could partly pay you back that way, Jim!"

"Steady," said Silver.

He had stripped off his clothes and wrung them in his powerful hands, the water spurting out in strong, muddy jets. Now he pulled on the damp things again. The wind still was blowing in gusts, not steadily. The rain rushed downward in great volleys. Sometimes drops fell hissing into the fire around which Silver had begun again to roast rabbit meat.

"We're comfortable enough here," said Silver. "And Christian is groaning now. He's lost you. His trap has been sprung, and the she-wolf is gone. Whisper, they call her. She's gone, and Frosty and she are hitting it for the tall timber somewhere, side by side. That means that Christian is as far as ever from your uncle's gold mine. He's lost Whisper, and that means that he's lost his first real chance at Frosty."

"What turned the she-wolf loose? I know they call her Whisper. What turned her loose?"

"I did. That's why I left you with Parade."

"Why didn't you kill her?" asked Gary. "They have the dogs, and the dogs still will know her scent. They ran her down before, and they'll run her down again. That pack will trail and catch any wolf in the world except Frosty. You should have killed her, chief."

Silver drew a long breath and shook his head ruefully.

"Perhaps I should," he admitted. "But just then it seemed to me that she'd won a right to run a little longer beside Frosty. Gold mine or no gold mine—cattle killing or not—Frosty has some of the makings of a gentleman, Alec. Anyway, Barry Christian is the worst wolf of the lot!"

CHAPTER XXII

Surrounded

IT rained all of seven days. It rained as the sky can only in the mountains. The winds held steadily in the north-west, carrying vast masses of water vapor in toward the heights, where the currents were forced upward, the mist congealed to drops, and mile-deep clouds disgorged their contents swiftly, continuously.

The sound of the rivers increased all through the land. The forests were sodden. The grasses were pale. A million little rivulets, running day and night, carried yellow detritus down the slopes, and in the ravines the creeks were white with eager speed, and the rivers they joined kept thundering with increasing voices.

There was rain by day and rain by night. Only now and again was there a pause as the clouds broke up for an hour or more. The lowlands were flooded. Worst danger of all, now and then a cloudburst filled a number of upper ravines all in an hour, and sent the contents hurtling down into the narrows of some greater valley, a wall of water, a great bore that whittled the trees off the banks, shaved away the banks themselves, reached out casual hands here and there, and flicked cabins and all their contents into the basins of the streams.

But all through this bad weather Frosty was the happiest wolf in the Rocky Mountains. On the night when his mate was delivered from the second mortal peril of her life, he had heard her howl of freedom, of release, and of yearning, and he had come to her as to a star. After that he had marched straight across the mountains, passing right out of his known range into strange country. He had turned the next day and come back into his own country, to a point a full thirty miles away from his former abode with his mate. And on that day he had found a young and foolish deer in the higher hills, and he had taught his mate the delightful game of deer hunting.

Wolves do the trick by knowing the habits of a deer, which runs full speed for a certain length of time, and then, if not followed closely, turns off the trail sharply to one side or the other, and is apt to lie down and try to make itself invisible in the woods until it has regained its breath.

The trick consists in spotting the deer and then posting a hunter at either end of the approximate course in which it is expected that the venison will run. Frosty was an old master of the art, not because he had had help before in doing the thing, but because he more than once had studied the devices of others of his kind from some high place, and had waited until the kill before he descended to rob the victors of their prize.

There was nothing that Frosty liked so much as meat that had been warmed for him by the labors of others!

Now he had a mate faster than himself on foot, though not so enduring, and, though she had not his brains, she was at least a good pupil and a faithful follower. So he took her down the valley, posted her, returned to the deer, and gave the animal a good flying start toward the she-wolf. That deer ran through the valley three miles like a raging wind. At the end of the three miles Whisper sprang up.

She headed the deer right back up the valley, and the hunted beast, with not a doubt that it was the same wolf

which, wing-footed, had managed to head her off, cam
hurling back up the valley, only to find big Frosty, fres
and well rested, all prepared for her.

She knew then that she had been tricked, and brok
straight up the valley slope to get to new ground; but si
miles of sprinting will kill the heart of even a strong deer
she lasted another five miles or so, with Frosty at he
heels. Then he cut her down, called Whisper, and woul
not taste a morsel until Whisper had come running up an
been received by his red laugh of welcome.

The deer was the beginning of a streak of good luc
and astute hunting which kept their larder filled, an
though Frosty kept thinking of the fat lowlands where th
scent of game was crossed by the odor of man and stee
he refrained from leading his mate down on another expe
dition. Her eyes were still uneasy. In her sleep she moane
and twitched her legs, still fleeing from man in he
dreams.

In the meantime, there was no sight, or sound, or sme
of the dog pack that had caught her once before, but o
the seventh day after her escape the keen ear of Frosty
which was always studying the sounds of the mountain
and dissolving them into their component parts, detecte
the baying of dogs.

He knew the hateful chorus and leaped to his feet. Hi
mate jumped to his side with her mane bristling. She hel
her head high, exactly like his, and then she made out th
gloomy music in the distance once more.

Her red length of tongue hung out. She began to pan
and with her shifting, bright eyes she searched for shelte
There would not be much run in her this time. Terro
would freeze up the strength of her limbs quickly; fea
would constrict her breathing.

So Frosty headed for the best water hazard that h
knew anything about.

Wolves don't like water, but neither do dogs. Frost
headed straight for the Purchase River, whose valley split
the Blue Waters in a long knife stroke. What Frosty wante
to do was to enter the current and swim down it a consid
erable distance until he would reach a series of low san

bars that ran out from the farther shore. There he could land and wade ashore into thick brush.

Twice before this he had shaken off persistent hunters after his scalp by the same maneuver, and though he was not one to duplicate his measures in times of need, he felt assured that this was the trick to get Whisper away from the dogs with the least expenditure of effort.

So he jogged overland with her. On the high verge of the Purchass ravine he paused and looked over the ragged mountains through which they had just come, and listened to the hateful singing of the dog pack far away. Then he took Whisper zigzagging down the side of the canyon to the flat ground beside the water.

The stream was high. It had swollen to such a degree that it was eating away the banks on both sides. Even as he watched, he saw a young willow tree topple, sink, and then whirl away down the creek.

That was a bad sign. When things whirled in running water it meant that there are undertows, cross-currents, all sorts of things that will pull down a wolf, no matter how strong a swimmer he may be. Frosty had almost drowned one day in water that to the casual eye seemed almost perfectly calm. That had taught him to watch with care the movement of anything that floated on the face of a stream before he ventured into it.

It had been his plan to take to the water almost at once, so as to make a greater gap between the point where he entered the creek and the place at which he left it.

Now he hesitated so long that at last he heard the cry of the dog pack open on the heights above him. That started him forward again.

He decided that he would run down around the bend where the creek was joined by two small tributaries and swelled out, at certain seasons of the year, into quite a river. So he headed forward with Whisper and turned the bend.

He was troubled even before he came in sight of the new picture. The air trembled with noises such as he had never heard in this valley before. Was it merely sound that worked on him, or was there really a slight shuddering of the rocks over which he ran?

Then he ran around the bend and had full view of a very strange picture indeed. The whole place was so changed that he could hardly recognize it. It filled him with fear to find such alteration. It was like dreaming a thing small and finding it big. The creek he had seen much swollen above its usual size, but it was nothing compared with the two tributaries which here joined the main channel. They came bounding out of their ravines like endless chains of wild/ horses, throwing heads and manes, and neighing all together on a deep note of thunder.

Seven days of steady rain had turned the trick. And still there were great black clouds to the northwest sweeping down to hide the tops of the mountains, pouring continual floods out of the sky. To carry away those floods the courses of the creeks hardly sufficed. They were crowded. Old banks had been ripped away. Still the throats of the creeks were gorged. The booming and the dashing noises were something hardly to be believed.

And the shallows where Frosty had trusted that he could land? Well, there was a good, big, fat-sided island below the junction a little distance, and now that island had been whittled away until it lifted a transparent streak of foliage only. Frosty could look right through the brush and the trees to the bright frothing of the water beyond.

But the noise was worse than the alteration of the scene. The noise stunned him. However, it was no time for hesitation now. If he could not use the river as a water hazard, he would have to foot it down the valley as fast as he could run, and then cut back up the slope as soon as the sheer rock cliffs diminished to angles that he could climb. There was a cave that tunneled through half a mile of darkness in the bosom of Thunder Mountain, and offered one small exit on the other side of the peak. He would take Whisper there. In the narrows of the dark passage he could fight off the dogs for a time, at least, and after Whisper was rested, he could go on again with her.

However, he was already very troubled as he turned down the stream once more, and it was then that danger rose up and struck against his eyes close by. For issuing out of a side pass a mile down the canyon came two riders, the sun flashing on their naked rifles!

Frosty bared his teeth in a snarl as he understood. They had divined, with their crafty human brains, that he was heading across country toward the valley of the Purchass. Therefore they had divided their forces. The dog pack, which was now sending its cry right down the ravine toward the fugitives, had stuck close to the scent. The two riders had taken horse and rifle by a short way to the lower valley, hoping to head off the fugitives.

And they had done it! On one side Frosty had the high, sheer face of the rock wall of the valley. Behind him came the dogs. Before him rode the riflemen.

On the other side there was the deadly rush and swirling of the water!

But the other three things meant certain death. The water was the least terrible choice of all. He hunched his shoulder against Whisper and forced her toward the brink of the stream. She flashed about at him, her eyes green with dangerous light, but in a moment she understood, and obediently, but trembling, stepped down into the stream.

The water was not very cold—but what force it had! It was tugging and pulling as though in anger before Frosty was knee-deep. However, it had to be endured. He stuck out his head and hurled himself forward in a long skimming dive. The water closed over him. A trick of the current started him rolling. He came up, thoroughly soaked, half blinded, and saw Whisper still tumbling and struggling in the same cross-catch of the water.

Now she righted, saw him, and tried to swim to him, with panic in her eyes. The currents caught her and thrust her away. She began to struggle blindly. So Frosty headed deliberately toward her, though she was closer to the shore; and up that shore came two riders, rifles ready, gesticulating. And from the head of the ravine ran the dog pack.

Well, those hunters would never get their dogs into such water as this—not even when the prey was in full sight!

Whisper, when Frosty was close to her, mastered her panic once more and struck out more steadily. They inched away from the bank. Sometimes the riffles of the water covered their heads. Sometimes the currents would catch at them and throw them bodily forward at great speed. Sometimes they tried to dodge as shooting logs, the wreckage from forest far back in the mountains, slid past them. Sometimes those logs were rolling rapidly. Sometimes the currents started Frosty rolling, too.

They had rounded the bend. The two riflemen were riding the bank, watching. It was strange that the shooting had not started!

It seemed certain that Frosty could not reach the head of the almost washed-out island. He would have to strike it somewhere on the flank.

Then he found a streak of white water that rushed him straight down past the entire length of the island and left him floundering, very tired and breathless, in the middle of the stream below the island. He knew that he could not swim back to either shore from that position. But there was one sudden hope that appeared before his eyes. Right down the stream, a half mile away, loomed the broad forehead of another island, rather close to the left bank. He might be able to make that point.

But another sight stunned and bewildered him a moment later. For on the left bank of the stream he saw two riders, and one of them sat on the back of a horse that shone like a statue of gold. Frosty was hemmed in on either side, before and behind. He felt that he had come at last to the day of his death.

CHAPTER XXIII

The Voice of Man

DESPAIR made Frosty stop swimming for a moment, and his mate, in that interval, moved past him with a steady stroke. She swam well, very well. She seemed to be less paralyzed with panic, when she was in the water, than she had been on the dry land. Frosty took heart at once and drew level with her.

Guns were firing across the river. Bullets were chipping, now, at the water through which he progressed, as though the men of the dog pack realized that there was some ghost of a chance that Frosty might reach the island and escape through the brush and the trees.

Other guns fired from the opposite bank, though none of those bullets struck the water.

Then the gunfire continued, but not a single slug of lead touched Frosty or the river water about him.

He discovered, when he raised his head for a glance around, that the men and the horses and the dogs all had disappeared behind shrubs or rocks on both sides of the river. The firing continued—but not at Frosty. Was it possible that the men were shooting at one another?

The brain of Frosty could not quite understand. But what he did understand was that though his body and his struggling legs were very tired, it no longer seemed impossible to reach the island. Despair left him. If he had had to swim the distance, he would have been lost, he knew, but his swimming was only a small assistance to the strong current that drove him straight on toward the island. It was not big. It was very low of land. It was covered with straggling brush and a few small trees. But to Frosty it looked finer than any delightful hunting lands that ever he had traveled in his life.

The shooting, whirling current that continually rolled him under was now a blessing. He was willing to submit to its buffeting, for it was throwing him toward his goal.

His mate had begun to tire badly. Now and again she turned her head slowly toward him, her body slewing around a little. But there was not far to travel. The water shoaled suddenly away. Before them the current was curling against rocks and some half-drowned shrubs. As the firm bottom came under his feet, Frosty found himself so tired that he could hardly lift his weight. The water seemed a familiar and helpful element now, and the air was hostile, giving no support whatever.

The she-wolf could hardly support herself. She went forward, wabbling and staggering, as bullets, in a sudden flight, sang through the air about them, bit the water, crackled through the brush, thudded against the rocks. The men from the dog pack had opened fire again!

Whisper got into the safety of the low brush. Frosty leaped after her, gathering his strength desperately for the effort. It was while he was in the air that a bullet from Barry Christian's rifle struck him. The slug went right through his hind quarters. He fell forward, sprawling.

There was not much pain. There was only a numbness, and his hind legs would not obey his will. They would not move. He lay in the brush bewildered. He turned his head and snapped at the air as though at a fly.

Whisper came up to him, whimpering, smelled his blood, drew back, and sat down to howl.

Then the pain began.

It started with the wound and ran down in cold electric shudderings to his hind toes. It thrust upward in hot grippings into his entrails. He knew as well as a man could have known that something ought to be done, but he could not tell what.

He wanted darkness, quiet, the stillness of a cave. So he dragged himself forward, working hard with his forelegs and pulling the weight of his body after him. He worked himself in this fashion through the brush and up a rise to the top of the only small eminence of land on the island.

Through gaps in the brush and the trees he could see the river on both sides of him. The water was running with a great, foaming rush toward the side of the river from which he had swum. On the other side the extent of the river was almost as great, but it seemed shallower, and the currents did not thrust with such boiling force. That was the side of the man with the golden horse, the man who had been twice so close to Frosty that by closing his eyes and shrinking his sensitive nostrils a little the wolf could remember him perfectly.

Whisper came and licked one of the wounds. She stood back, shaking her head like a doctor that gives up a case. For the blood kept on welling out. Frosty half closed his eyes and sniffed at the wound in his turn. The blood kept on coming. It had a hot smell. He knew the scent of his own blood, and that scent was sickening to him. It brought cold fear into his heart.

He lay still. His heart was beating rapidly, shaking his body against the ground. And the pain was terrible. It ate at his nerves, corroded his strength and courage, made him want to howl the death song. But he kept the voice back. He had learned the value of silence.

He kept his eyes shut. He wanted darkness, and felt that in the black of the night everything might be well for him.

Then Whisper came, with a snarl humming in the back of her throat. She was stiff on her toes, her mane ruffing up; she looked exactly as though she were going to attack him, but then he followed the direction in which her head pointed, and he was able to see, through the brush,

139

that the golden stallion had been ridden down into the river. It was swimming with powerful strokes toward the island, and the man was with it.

Man was coming—and for Frosty there was no further flight! He lifted his fore quarters, but the agony that ran through his hind legs was so great that he had to lie down again. His red eyes commenced to blink, as though he were facing a powerful light; death was, in fact, what he was confronting.

He lost sight of the swimmers when they were close to the island; presently Whisper, with a whimper, slunk away through the brush. Noises of cracklings through the shrubbery approached. The wind brought the odor of man, of *the* man. With it was the smell of the wet horse, of gunpowder, and of steel. Shudderings went through Frosty. He lifted his head, turned it toward the enemy, and waited. His short ears pricked up. There was nothing to tell that he was in a panic of terror. There was nobility in Frosty, and therefore, when the pinch came, he knew how to face death.

And so, through the brush, came the image of the man, shadowy, broken across by the small branches, and at last standing in clear day before Frosty. Frosty locked his jaws.

"A dead one!" said Jim Silver. Then he added: "Poor devil!"

He walked around the great wolf, staring at the ground. Frosty disdained to turn his head to watch. He would not even strain to look out of the corners of his eyes. For, of course, the man would do what Frosty would have done —go behind and take a helpless enemy from the blind rear.

It was better to lie like that, head up and neck rigid, pretending not to see or hear, pretending all was a pleasant daydream. Presently a gun would speak.

"Where's your mate, Frosty?" said the voice of the man. "Has she run off?"

It was a strange sound. The vibration of the human voice ran all through the body of Frosty, along with his pain. He had heard human voices many a time before, but never a voice with such a quality in it. There was in it something that he vaguely recognized as kindness. When his mother spoke in the cave in the ancient days, or when she had scolded and warned in the days of his cub hunting, there had been a touch of the same quality in the tone. Frosty recognized it only vaguely. There is no kindness from an enemy. For enemies one has a sharp tooth. It is the law of the wild. And no tooth is as sharp as the tooth of man, no mercy is so small as his.

Well, the end was coming.

"Bleeding very fast—bleeding to death!" said Jim Silver.

He walked around to the front of Frosty, pulled out a revolver, and leveled it. Silver was wet and wringing with water. It coursed down him in small rivulets, and the sun, looking out from between a pair of clouds, turned him to a form of fire bright as the flame of a hearth, bright as the sun on still water.

But Frosty did not blink his eyes at the brightness or at the death which was leveled at him. He kept his head high. His great heart was swelling in him. His jaws were locked. He had turned himself into steel to meet the end.

"I can't do it," said Jim Silver.

His voice had been like a hiss. He lowered the gun.

Now, if Whisper had brains and courage together, she might steal out of the brush where she lurked and take the man from behind, cutting him down by the legs or striking at the back of the neck. But Whisper would not do that!

It was strange to see the gun lower in the hand of the man. Perhaps, of course, man intended to play with him, prolonging the agonies of his death.

Well, that was permitted, also. That was another law of the realm. And Frosty remained like a rock.

"I don't think you'll even fight," said Jim Silver. "I think the fight's out of you, because you won't make a fool of yourself in a lost cause."

He walked around behind Frosty and came right up to his hind quarters. Frosty didn't move. He might wrench himself around with a great effort and strike with his fangs at the enemy, but it was likely to be a futile blow.

He lay still. There was a rending sound, loud and sharp in the air. Jim Silver was tearing clothes into long strips for a bandage. Under a thick bush he found some deep, dry dust. He came back with some of the dust and crouched right over Frosty; and Frosty would not turn his head. Pain had nailed him to the ground—pain and helplessness. Oh, if the four feet were under him, how quickly he would have slashed for the softness of the throat of terrible man —and then how he would have rushed away for safety! How he would have whipped through the brush to rejoin Whisper, to plunge again into the water!

But the voice of man kept on speaking. It was like the flowing of a stream. A strange kindness kept soaking out of it and into the mind and heart of Frosty. It was the caress before the death stroke, no doubt!

Then a bandage was worked under Frosty's hind quarters. A handful of dust was laid over the mouth of one wound to clot the blood. The bandage was drawn tight and tighter. It was painful only in the first moment. After that the pressure was soothing. It pulled the lips of the wound together. And Frosty knew that the blood was no longer flowing from that open mouth, dribbling his life away.

Then the wise hands of man turned him. Ah, that was an agony, to be sure. Frosty dropped his head suddenly and let it rest on his paws. The second bandage was passed under him; the second handful of dust was laid over the mouth of that more gaping wound where the bullet had issued from the flesh. The bandage drew tight with a pang that seemed to split the very heart of Frosty. His head whipped around like the head of a snake, at inescapable speed, and he caught the arm of Jim Silver in his teeth.

CHAPTER XXIV

A Partner

IT was that famous right hand of Silver that was endangered. But it was not yet lost. A wolf usually strikes with his teeth as a man strikes with a sword—a gashing blow with the point, or the edge. But something had checked Frosty in the last instant, and he only gripped the arm in a vice, without breaking the skin. Red hatred blurred his eyes, but still they could see clearly enough, and if Jim Silver had moved a hand or twitched so much as a muscle, the fangs of Frosty would have crunched against the bone. There would have been an end of Silver indeed, a crippled wreck that his enemies could have devoured soon with consummate ease.

But all that Silver stirred was his voice, that kept on in the steady stream, and softened the fighting rage of Frosty, and sank again into his brain, into his heart.

There was neither fear nor anger in the eyes of Jim Silver. Those were calm, all-watchful, brooding eyes, considering the wolf and understanding him.

He was not even calling himself a fool for taking the chance. He had had no rope with him to tie down the brute, and unless something were done, the life would rapidly leak out of that great body.

Why not let the life run away? Well, that would be an easy question to ask. It would have been easily answered, also, Jim Silver felt, by any man who had seen Frosty fighting for his mate, by any man who saw him waiting calmly, head high, for his death.

Big shudders of weakness ran through the body of Frosty. Suddenly he relaxed his hold and let the right hand of Jim Silver go, but he kept his head turned and ready, and waiting to strike one of those wise hands to the bone.

Yes, with a tooth he had scratched the skin, and not for the first time the taste of the blood of man was sweet in his mouth. A hot slaver overflowed the lips of Frosty and drooled down from his mouth. The green devil was bright in his eyes once more. Urges kept rushing over him in waves, and a thin thread was all that held him back. And the voice of man continued gently in the ears and in the brain of Frosty.

The sound of it or the memory of it would never leave him. It would be present in his soul from that day forward, and make of the neighborly mountains a solitude for him where he had always reigned supreme as a king.

But Frosty could not know that. Such things were working in him as never had troubled him before. And always there was the emotion that had never been in him since the days when his mother ran with her litter, giving them gentleness and care. But this? It was beyond all the laws of kind!

The hands of man pressed the dust over the wound again slowly. The red blood soaked into it, clotted it, appeared through it as a thin stain. More dust was heaped on. It was incredibly soft on the raw flesh. As the bandages were drawn again there was, as before, one thrust of pain, and after that there followed such a release from torment that the breathing of Frosty began to make a steady sound, like snoring.

The second bandage was drawn tight in that manner. The pain continued, but only a ghost of its old self. The bleeding had stopped. The life drain no longer carried away the strength of Frosty on a steady ebb.

The hand of man moved out to him. He smelled it with a keenly critical nose. The scent of his own blood and hair and hide was thick on it. He had suddenly no desire to strike that hand.

Good had been done him. He could not understand. He could only feel and know that good had flowed out to him from those hands. The gentleness of the voice was not a liar. There was other tenderness in this world than in the care of a mother wolf.

The hand went straight on toward his eyes. Frosty snarled so that his entire body vibrated. The hand hung suspended in the air. He stopped snarling. The hand moved toward him again. Once more he snarled. A wild burst of savagery almost mastered him, weakened, ebbed away from its full tide.

What is there to fear or hate in a thing that can be stopped by a mere growl?

He let the hand touch him, and it rested with weight and with warmth on the top of his head.

If it covered his eyes, he would rend the arm. He would catch it in the softness of the flesh beneath the elbow, and he would tear it. He would slash through the big blood vessels, and with his wrenching tug of head and shoulders he would jerk the man closer and then get at the tenderness of the throat.

The whole body of man was tender, easily rent by teeth. Frosty could tell that. Jim Silver was naked to the waist now, after turning his clothes into bandages. The teeth of Frosty tingled with eagerness as he saw game so easy. And if his eyes were covered for an instant—

He waited, teeth bared, silent. But his eyes were not covered. The hand passed down his head, softly, steadily. The voice went on, always running through the heart of Frosty as the sound of running water passes into the heart of a thirsty wolf on a summer's day.

But the thirst which was beginning in Frosty on this day might never be assuaged.

The voice of Jim Silver was saying softly: "Now that

145

I've got my hand on your head you're mine. I'll have you coming to my voice, watching me at night, following my shadow, waiting for my step, listening for my voice. I'll make you mine from the tip of your tail to the light in your eyes. Frosty, you've found a partner. I'll belong to you from my toes to my brain. We'll work together, travel together, hunt together and fight the same enemies. Oh, it'll be a wise man who can keep his trail from me now. I won't have to trust my eyes, but your nose. I won't have to see in the dark, because I'll have you with me. You to show me the way, Parade to carry me—and Barry Christian has come very close to his last day!"

He slipped his hand down the neck of the wolf to the collar and unbuckled it. As he was withdrawing the bright weight, impulse made Frosty grip the arm of the man again.

But this time he retained his hold for only a moment. He let that arm go free, and saw the man stand up and away from him.

Consider this with the brain of a wolf. All men in the world shoot bullets at wolves—all saving one.

All men try to run them down with horses and catch them in ropes—all men save one.

All men seed the earth with traps, so that the fleshless jaws may grip a wolf by the leg—all men save one.

But from the hands of one man there comes the easing of pain, the sound of a voice that causes courage and confidence to course through the heart.

Frosty lay still, with his head stretched on the ground. All that he was aware of it would be impossible to say, but most of all he knew that strange eyes had been on him, taking hold of his brain.

Big Jim Silver had the little compartment of the collar open now. He took out a twist of stained, oiled silk. He spread out the paper that it contained and commenced reading:

Thunder Mountain on the right; Chimney Peak on the left. I face Mount Wigwam. A ledge of black rock—

There was blood on the paper. That was the blood of Bill Gary, and it was still red.

Silver read the directions again, printed them deep in his mind. But in the meantime there was Alec Gary to be considered, for to him the gold should belong.

He took from a pocket of his torn coat a bit of pencil and wrote beneath the sprawling writing of the dead man:

Go and get men to help you. I inclose two hundred dollars to pay them their hire. Go to the spot that your uncle described, locate the mine, and register your claims. I am staying on here. Don't ask me why. I'll see you when I have a chance. Don't wait for me until the flood sinks. I'm not leaving this spot for a good many days.

JIM SILVER.

After he had written that, he got his water-soaked wallet, counted out the money, wrapped it with the note inside the oiled silk, and found that he was barely able to inclose the whole within the compartment in the collar.

Then he walked down through the trees to the edge of the river and waved his hand. There was an instant signal from behind a rock on the farther shore, some thirty yards away. For here the secondary channel of the stream deepened and narrowed. It was Alec Gary who ventured to show himself, though cautiously. For the men of Barry Christian were beyond the island.

Jim Silver took a step forward, swung his arm, and hurled the heavy collar high and far. It flattened out in the air. It spun around and around, flashing like a straight sword. And it fell actually beyond Alec Gary.

Alec ran back to it, leaned over it.

A moment later he was dancing like a madman, flinging up his arms.

Silver, smiling a little, turned slowly back through the brush. He felt that the proper half was being fitted to that interrupted day which had been broken through by the death of Bill Gary. And once again fortune had evaded the skillfully grasping hands of Barry Christian.

CHAPTER XXV

Flood Waters

SILVER carried on his saddle a small hand ax with an adjustable and folding handle of steel tubing. He used that ax to fell some boughs and saplings. He made a deep bed, piled it beside the wounded wolf, leaned over Frosty, and lifted him onto the bed.

That is one way of telling it.

Another way is to admit that it took him twenty-four hours of persuading, stroking, talking, trying, before he was permitted to take the massive, loose weight of the big wolf in his arms and lift it onto the evergreen boughs.

Once he had that bed under Frosty he had some assurance that the big fellow might get well eventually.

In the meantime he had to get food. But that was not a hard task. There were plenty of rabbits on the island. Before flood time it was twenty times as large as the surface now above water, and therefore twenty times as much life as usual was crowded onto its face. There were plenty of rabbits. There were plenty of snakes, too. After he discovered the numbers of them, Silver dared not venture into the woods except by day, and then only with the very greatest care.

But he got a rabbit for the wolf and another for himself the first day.

The great Frosty would not even sniff at meat killed by another than himself. He merely turned his head and looked at the glorious figure of Parade, where the stallion grazed at the side of the clearing. This was the sort of fodder that Frosty had a taste for.

Jim Silver brought up water in his hat. Frosty would not even glance at it, though terrible thirst burned him.

So Silver waited another day. He understood the thing perfectly, but there was nothing to do about it.

He waited three days before Frosty, lying faint and dying, deigned to accept water from the hat.

He waited another whole day, though famine made the ribs of the wolf stare, before Frosty, with snarling, disgusted lips, bared his teeth and bit into a rabbit.

But he ate one rabbit that day and two the next—rabbits freshly killed, warm with life still, as a proper wolf demands to have his food. And so he passed that important event—the taking of food which he had not killed with his own fangs.

The days went on. The bandages were changed, re-changed, again and again. Water was heated in the hollow of a rock and the wounds washed. They were healing swiftly, but still Frosty was too wise to attempt to move, for deep inside him there were torn tendons, ripped flesh, and grazed bones. He lay still and accepted the attendance of the man.

Silver used to come and put a hand on his head and look straight down into his eyes.

"I serve you to-day, and you serve me to-morrow," he would say.

But there was never much sign from Frosty. He had the forbidding exterior which is fitting for a king. It was a startling revelation to Jim Silver when the first token of affection was given.

He had torn his hand on a thorn, a deep and ragged wound, and as he was offering the great wolf a freshly

149

killed rabbit that day, Frosty turned from the meat to the raw wound on the hand of Silver and licked it carefully, gently, with his eyes half closed.

Not until he seemed to think that that small hurt had received sufficient attention would Frosty start eating. To Silver it was like a miracle. He knew from that moment how strong his hold on the wolf had become.

Then bad luck struck at them again. The storm no longer touched the island even with its outer fringe. There had been days of clear, open weather. But up in the higher mountains of the northwest, still the thick haze of the rains continued. A flood piled up, rushed out of the smaller canyons, and raised the Purchass River five feet in five minutes. That water sent down a solid wall that traveled as fast as a trotting horse. It hit the island and literally tore away the head of it. The big trees were ripped out by the roots with a sound like thunder-clouds tearing in two. And a shooting wave of water came up over the hillock on which Parade and Silver and the wounded wolf had been living.

And Whisper crawled out from the brush, more afraid of the raging water than of man. She lay down at the side of Frosty, crouching herself small against him, and showing her needle-sharp teeth to Silver. She was not the only thing that came. Half a dozen rattlesnakes came sliding and slipping away from the flood, and never sounded the alarm once when they came to other living things.

The water was deep, and had a current. Silver saddled Parade, got on him, and then hauled up Frosty to keep him from the wet. Silver would never forget that moment. For it was the real introduction of Parade to Frosty. The loathing between them was perfect. And now the wolf lay on the back of the stallion, snarling with hate, and shivering with the blood lust, while Parade quaked with horror under the weight of the beast of prey.

The wall of water receded. It left the island pretty well ruined, and very much smaller. Whisper sneaked first of all away from the hillock to go back to her rabbit hunting, and her noisy mourning for the fellowship of Frosty by night. The rattlesnakes slithered away through the brush, and Silver was able to continue his life as before.

There were no dull moments. It was true that Frosty could not move his hind quarters, but his head was free. He might never rise and walk again, but he was able to use his mind. And Silver worked it constantly. With all of Frosty's wisdom and savage cunning and myriad cruelties, he had the heart of a happy puppy. He liked a game as well as a murder.

He learned to catch a rock or a stick. He got so that he could catch a ten-pound chunk of wood thrown from short range about as hard as Silver could fling it. Frosty's snaky head would dart out to meet the flying weight, and with a side twist of his head and his supple, strong neck, he would break the shock of the impact. He could catch the same lump when it was tossed high in the air above his head. He learned, also, a complicated vocabulary of signs and gestures and words and whistles.

Sometimes, as Silver ran through their antics together, the eyes of Frosty would brighten and dance, his head went high, and he looked like a dog about to bark. But when his throat swelled and his body shook with the desire to utter some pleasant sound, all he could bring out was a horrifying growl.

Frosty lay there for many long days before Silver saw him stand. There was no preparation; there was no warning, no elaborate approach to the feat. But Silver opened his eyes one morning and saw the great wolf on his feet and tottering toward the brush. He started as Silver stood up, and Frosty looked around at him green-eyed, with a hideous snarl.

Silver merely laughed at him. He went up to Frosty and patted his head. He got to work on the hind legs and massaged them carefully. And in three more days Frosty was walking freely and easily. After that his strength came back to him with a rush.

He was with Whisper at night, but all the day long he was with Silver. The reason was that there was always something to occupy his attention when he was with the man. There were endless games. Among the trees, high in the branches, or in some nest of rocks, Silver would hide

151

himself and give the signal for the hunt with one thin whistle. And always Frosty worked out the most complicated trail problem in a few moments and sat down with his red laughter in front of his man.

Frosty learned how to flush game, how to work through the brush to make the rabbits come scattering out before the gun of man, where they would surely fall. He learned how to take the reins of Parade and lead him, Parade shuddering with horror, and the wolf with fighting rage. He learned how to fetch and carry, how to hear a whisper and obey it.

When Frosty seemed to have four strong legs under him at last, Jim Silver got on Parade and forded the river at the shallows, for the water had sunk far after the last flood. Frosty followed him over. Frosty followed him right on to the town of Blue Waters, and there he sat down on a hill and canted his head to one side as Silver continued into the place. Whisper came sneaking out and tried to draw her mate back into the woods, away from the fatal and strange trail of man, and Jim Silver, glancing over his shoulder, saw her trying her wiles.

But he let her have her way and went on into the town.

The news of Alec Gary's gold strike would be in everybody's mouth, of course. There had been plenty of time for Alec to reach the mine, locate it, file his claim, and start taking out the dust from the rock. There had been plenty of time for Alec to do all of these things and finally to go back up the Purchass River to a certain island where he had last seen Jim Silver—the Jim Silver who had placed a fortune in his hands.

Perhaps Alec would be glad to forget all about Jim Silver's aid. There was grim curiosity in the heart of Silver as he started to make inquiries.

But in five minutes he was something more than curious. For Alec Gary had never got to the town of Blue Waters on the day when he left Jim Silver. Not a man in the town had seen him; certainly he had not appeared to hire men or to file a claim!

What had become of him? Silver knew the answer. Barry Christian had blocked the way!

CHAPTER XXVI

The Search

SILVER went back to the hill where he had left Frosty, and found the great wolf lying exactly where he had been at first; off through the brush, with a thin sound of rustling, went Whisper.

Silver, looking Frosty in the eye, wondered how long the charm would last. Wolves, most people said, could never be tamed. They would revert to the wild. But for the short time that this companionship might endure—so long, perhaps, as the memory of his recent wounds was fresh in the head of Frosty—it was a wonderful thing to Silver. And he sat there by the wolf, smoking a cigarette and working out his plan.

Alec Gary had been in a frenzy of excitement when he received the words of his uncle. No doubt he had mounted his horse and ridden like mad straight for the town of Blue Waters. He *could* not have had any other destination. He would have gone on a straight line. And what would that straight line have been?

Silver charted it in his mind, and then rode it on Parade,

with Frosty running on ahead, hunting sights and sounds, reading the scents that traveled the wind.

The way from Blue Waters to the island on the Purchass River cut straight across high land, and skirted the head of a box canyon where a creek tumbled noisily over a sheer wall of rock. Or if Gary were not familiar with the country, he might have cut straight across the canyon without skirting the head of it; the slopes on either side were not at all difficult. So Silver rode down into the canyon.

There was nothing in the little valley worth looking at except the scattered bones of a horse that were whitening in the sun. Silver would have ridden on, except that Frosty poked into a patch of thick shrubbery and turned back to eye his master until Silver came to the place.

There he found something that was worth while indeed. It was the battered wreckage of a range saddle which was ripped and torn as if it had been passed through a mill. A mill with water in it, to judge by the way the sun had curled and warped the tattered fragments of the leather. But what mattered most to Jim Silver was the way some of the saddle strings had been knotted. By those knots, he knew that it was the saddle of Alec Gary that he was seeing!

Those bones, then, were the bones of Alec's horse; and Alec himself?—well, his body could have been concealed anywhere about the valley. There were a thousand rock piles in any one of which he might have been buried, while Barry Christian, and Gregor, and Thurston, armed with the secret of the mine, went straight to their quarry!

Silver went there, too. He spent a day getting to Thunder Mountain, and locating, by means of Chimney Peak and Mount Wigwam, the ledge of black stone. He found the broken place where Bill Gary had blasted away the outer part of the ledge. He saw the rich glistening of the gold itself, but there was no token that any one had been working the mine.

Alec Gary might be as dead as his horse, but apparently Christian had not stolen his secret!

Back to the ravine of the dead horse and the saddle went Jim Silver, and spent another day going over it from the bottom to the head. Frosty helped him hunt, not that

Frosty knew what was wanted, but because it was plain to him that man was hunting; so, while Frosty worked here and there, calling attention to a dead bird here, and a nest of mice there, Whisper lurked on the edge of the horizon all day, and came close at night with mournful howlings.

It was on the evening of the last day of the search that Frosty himself howled short and sharp from the head of the valley, and Silver saw him sitting on a ridge just under the waterfall. He climbed to the place. There was not much to be seen—just one spot staining the whiteness of the rock, and one little sparkling point of metal from which Frosty lifted the foot he had placed on it. Silver picked the thing up and started, for it was the rowel of a spur that had been broken from its wheel.

That stain on the rock, to judge by the bristling of the wolf as he sniffed it, might be blood. Then, had horse and rider fallen here from the edge of the height above? Had the rider struck on the ledge while the horse, toppling farther out, had dashed down onto the boulders of the creek and been swept along in the water to the point where unknown hands had pulled it out from the stream, stripped off the saddle, and dropped the saddle for hiding into the brush?

What people would have done those things? Who except Barry Christian and his crew; and might not their rifle bullets have been the cause of the fall in the first place?

Frosty had run off down the ledge, sniffing here and there at a dabbling of other spots on the rock. Silver followed. The trail led up from the ledge to the level above, and worked a short distance over the gravel before Frosty had to give it up. After all, it was many days old.

Silver could merely take the general direction and follow it. For perhaps Alec, when he was hurt by his fall, had managed to get rid of the paper that contained the secret of the mine's position. Perhaps he had been picked up by Christian and carried to some spot where he could be properly "persuaded" to talk about the situation of the mine.

At any rate, Silver rode a mile into the trees, paused, circled widely and vainly for sign, and then was forced to camp for the night. He was up with the dawn, and searching again. And in the bright, cool prime of the morning he came out into a clearing before a little trapper's shack and saw a grizzled old fellow seated in a chair that had been rudely fashioned out of the stump of a tree. He puffed at a clay pipe and greeted Silver with a grunt.

He had seen nothing of any stranger, he said. He knew nothing. He wanted to know nothing.

While he was still uttering his denials, a strained voice cried inside the shack: "Chimney Peak—I face Mount Wigwam—"

"That's the man I want!" said Silver.

The trapper stood up with a shotgun in his hands.

"There's been some mean skunks on his trail, whoever he is," he said. "Maybe you're one of 'em. Back up, son. I ain't slaved over that kid all these days to chuck him away to the first gent that comes askin' for him. Who are you?"

"Jim Silver," he answered.

"The devil you are," said the trapper. "And I'm Napoleon, eh? Pull off your hat, if you're Jim Silver."

His glance shifted, at the same moment, to the shining beauty of that famous horse, Parade. Then, as Silver obediently removed his hat, the trapper stared at the little gray spots above the temples, like incipient horns. And he exclaimed:

"By thunder, you *are* Jim Silver. Come on inside this place and see what we can do for the kid. He's better, but he ain't well!"

Not well? No, he lay like a pale ghost of himself, all the upper part of his face bone-white and frightfully thin, and all the lower half of his face black with beard. But he heard the voice of Silver, and it made him sit up suddenly and throw out both hands in a great gesture of appeal. Silver took hold of one of those hands and sat down beside the bed. And there he remained day after day until the fever wore out of Alec Gary.

When he could tell his story, it was very simple. He had, as Silver suspected, ridden like a madman, straight for Blue Waters to get good men and take them to the mine. And on the way, as he climbed his horse up the highlands, Barry Christian and Gregor had appeared in his rear, riding hard.

156

Gary had fled. His mustang had held out well, but as he was passing near the head of the box canyon, a rifle bullet had knocked the mustang sprawling. Right over the edge of the cliff it had fallen, while Gary, with broken bones and torn body, lay by the grace of chance on the ledge close to the falls.

Christian and Gregor, riding down into the valley, had dragged the body of the horse out of the stream; perhaps had taken for granted that the body of the rider had simply disappeared in the water, lodged under some projecting rock. Perhaps, like Jim Silver, they had not even seen the little cross-ledge near the falls.

All that day, after his fall, Gary had not dared to move, though he felt himself dying. But in the night he had dragged himself up from the ledge and managed to get into the trees. There the trapper had found him, quite out of his wits with fever, the morning after.

It had been a hard job to pull him through. But cracked ribs will mend; mountain air breathes strength into the blood; and it was not many days after that before Jim Silver sat on a fallen tree and looked down a great slope to the place where the black ledge crossed the mountain, and where men were now moiling and toiling with a great clangoring of single jacks and double jacks against the drill heads. Young Alec Gary was in charge, walking here and there, by far the happiest man in the world.

Not that he claimed all the mine for himself. No; he wanted to give to Jim Silver half of the place, at least. Whatever Jim Silver would take was his. All of it, Gary swore, really should go to the only man in the world who could have checkmated Barry Christian.

But Silver, staring down the mountainside, found himself not altogether pleased by the clamoring that broke the gigantic peace of the uplands.

He whistled softly, and something stirred in the brush behind him. Without turning his head, he smiled. For he knew perfectly well that it was Frosty.

He pulled an envelope from his pocket and scribbled on the back of it:

DEAR ALEC: I'm going on. I have Frosty, and you have the mine. I can't take any part of it because there's blood on it—Bill Gary's blood. He died trying to pass the mine on to you, not to me. Now you have what he wanted you to have. It would only be bad luck for me, if I should take a slice.

I'm saying good-by this way because otherwise I know that I'd have an argument with you. So long and good luck.   JIM SILVER.

He put the envelope on a rock, weighted it with a stone, and climbed on Parade. Frosty jumped out of the brush, and, with a meaning toss of the head, led the way across the mountain to a small clearing, where Jim Silver saw the bones of huge dogs, or wolves, scattered on the pine needles. There were several rusted traps, and the teeth of one still held the hind leg bone of one of the dead.

Frosty, sitting down on the edge of the clearing, could not be persuaded even by all the coaxing of his master to put foot inside the place. So at last Silver rode on with Parade.

His way led north and west, through those mountains from which the floods had been rolling down so steadily not long before. As he rode, the big wolf, Frosty, took the way before him and seemed to guess at the direction in which his master was traveling.

Right through the day they journeyed, and in the evening, as they went down a valley, the voice of Whisper cried sadly from the height behind them.

Frosty put himself right across the trail and faced Silver. And Silver understood in this an ultimatum—that the bounds of Frosty's range had been crossed; that his mate would not leave the right domain; that Jim Silver, if he wished to keep the wolf, must stay in the wolf's land.

Silver understood, and without one word of persuasion, one call, one appeal, he rode Parade straight past Frosty and down into the thickening darkness of the lower valley.

There he camped in a thicket of big trees, and it seemed to him for the first time in years that it was a lonely thing to live with a horse alone in the wilderness. It seemed to him, as he sat dozing by the small fire, his chin on his fist, that he would give a great deal to have the wise head and the hazel eyes of the wolf to look at again. However, he felt that it was better this way. The wolf could not leave his kind. And after all, to live with any man was to live in bondage.

Then, lifting his heavy eyes, Silver saw a monstrous form sitting opposite him, with the firelight making a sheen of the eyes.

"Frosty!" he exclaimed. "Have you left her, son? Have you come to me?"

And Frosty looked up into the mysterious face of man and laughed his red laughter. For he was content.